Anonymous

Kosmos

The hope of the world

Anonymous

Kosmos
The hope of the world

ISBN/EAN: 9783337086695

Printed in Europe, USA, Canada, Australia, Japan

Cover: Foto ©Andreas Hilbeck / pixelio.de

More available books at **www.hansebooks.com**

KOSMOS

THE HOPE OF THE WORLD

THE HOPE OF THE WORLD

καλὸν γὰρ τὸ ἆθλον καὶ ἡ
ἐλπὶς μεγάλη.
Phaedo. § 145.

KOSMOS.

DRAMATIS PERSONÆ.

WALTER.

FELIX, *Walter's Son.*

ERIC, *a Philosopher.*

A Musician.

KOSMOS, *the Soul of the World.*

"WHOSOEVER has become thoughtful or melancholy through his own mishaps or those of others . . . whoever has known 'the pangs of despised love, the insolence of office, or the spurns which patient merit of the unworthy takes ;' he who has felt his mind sink within him, and sadness cling to his heart like a malady, who has had his hopes blighted, and his youth staggered by the apparition of strange things, who cannot be well at ease while he sees evil hovering about him like a spectre, . . . he to whom the universe seems infinite, and himself nothing, whose bitterness of soul makes him careless of consequences . . . this is the true Hamlet."—HAZLITT'S *Characters of Shakespeare's Plays.*

INTRODUCTION.

WALTER had held a high official appointment in the administration of a disaffected province, and had been successful in bringing forward a scheme for remedial legislation, and in restraining the populace from committing any overt act of hostility to the Government.

Unfortunately, however, just at the critical moment, a collision took place between the military and the people, which was followed by a general rising throughout the province. The revolt was speedily suppressed, and public opinion was quieted by making a scapegoat of Walter, who was required to resign, and who learned that the fact of his having been in communication with the popular leaders had given rise to strong suspicion as to his complicity with their designs.

Finding himself without a friend at court, and knowing that he had been marked down for assassina-

tion by the insurgents, for having as they thought
deceived them, Walter, broken in health, in fortune,
and in hope, retired with his only son, Felix, under
an assumed name, to a distant seaport ; and they
have lived there for a year when the scene opens.

KOSMOS.

ACT I

DE PROFUNDIS.

Scene I.—Walter's *study*.

Wal. How weary is my life ! Could I but sleep
And wake forgetful, or awake no more !
But rest I cannot ; and as one who falls
From mountain heights, and down the long white
    slope
Crashes, yet lives ; so from my pride of place
Have I been hurtled, and my mind is sore
And bruised, and all its fibres ache and burn
At touch of memory. My life has passed
Like running water, no one heeds my loss ;
My place is filled, betraying not a trace
Of all my projects. Did I ever live ?
I almost doubt it. Yet I laid my plans
So carefully ! None other than myself
Knew every detail of the vast machine,

Wheels within wheels, the lever framed to start
The giant arms in motion, or arrest
Their course at fitting moment.   So complete
Was my prevision, my design so clear,
Such perfect knowledge had I of the end
Before us, and its path, that present needs
I turned to future opportunities,
Making our policy suggest itself.
'Twas ours to deal with factions, diverse creeds,
An alien nobility, new laws
Transplanted from a more propitious soil,
Increasing burdens, and decreasing wealth : ·
And out of these discordant elements
I framed a bond of common interest,
Appealing here to hopes, and there to fears.
And, harder task, no jealousy I roused
Within the council ; there I kept aloof
From controversy, claiming not mine own,
Content for others to efface myself.
In short, although ' my Lords ' within my hands
Were puppets, yet I made them speak and move
As if by nature, aiding each so well
To play the part wherein he most excelled,
That no one saw his leading-strings, or knew
The unobtrusive hand that shaped his course.

Pshaw ! how bombastic does my vaunt appear;
And yet I thought it true.   Perchance 'twas I

Who cherished dreams, not they.   Full time to wake,
Yet hard the waking !   All my card-built house
Had fallen at a breath.   No proof had I
Of influence or merit.   Thoughts and words
Lacking protection, are like creatures wild,
Fair game for all.   My counsel and control
Were clean forgotten when my sun had set ;
Only routine remembered.

     " Yes, 'twas true.
I had been very useful—in my place ;
A mine of information ; they could wish
No better Secretary."

     Then I turned
For proofs, to my devotion in the cause
Of law and order ; to the love of right
Which filled my soul, leaving no room for self.
"Well, they had always liked me ;—yet, to speak
Truth, there were certain whispers that my aims
Were secret, and the facts too well confirmed
The worst suspicions ! "

     So I held my peace,
Eating my heart in secret.   Time passed on ;
And as I learned to think impartially,
Then not too hardly could I judge ' my Lords,'
Who only took me at my word.   What clue
Had they to trace the motives of a man
So blind to his advantage as myself?

Now came the hardest blow of all. For once
In conversation, when my course was blamed
For not insisting on a leading part,
Content to act as prompter, thankless task,
Unwittingly I said, " You see what comes
Of playing Providence !" And so we turned
To other subjects ; but in after days
That glared as though they never could grow dark,
And nights that mocked the promising of morn,
I vexed myself with questioning my words.
" Is Providence a person, or a term
Epitomizing universal law ? "
And first I answered, " Mind is lord of all,
And personal." I thought my faith in God
Was firmly anchored ; till beneath the stress
Of deep emotion, strong as ebbing tide,
It broke its moorings, drifting out to sea.
It drifted thus.
               " Does Mind reveal itself
To Mind ? "
                 Not so ! For if my friends were blind,
Failing to trace the art which made my plans
Most skilful when they seemed most natural ;
How much the more must Authorship Divine
Surpass discerning, hid behind the veil
Of perfect nature, seeming self-evolved ?
" Has Nature, then, no evidence of God ? "
None, where the mind is thoroughly imbued

With sympathy for **universal** law ;
For then unbroken seems the endless chain
Of Evolution through organic form
Whose natural selection shapes itself.
Each **act of** failure serving for the proof
Of general perfection.   All which yield
Beneath the tension of relentless strife
Return to the great crucible of Death ;
But each that stands the **test** of life, becomes
A link in the vast continuity
Of Nature, where success alone survives.
And surely 'tis not thus that perfect Mind
Its **instruments** would choose ; no need, **I ween.**
For Knowledge absolute, to cast aside
A thousand wasted seeds, that one may bear
More perfect fruit ; a wasted seed am I ;
And Nature's method less approves itself
Than once, when **I and** Nature were at one.
Token there is not, **nor** can ever be,
Of God in Nature, save, perchance, to those,
The fortunate, to whom their own success
Bears witness of beneficent design.

" What proof have the unfortunate of God ?
Wonders and signs ? "   No proofs are these to me ;
Poor comfort when I look for present help
To know the age of miracles has passed !
" That troubles are the punishment of sin ? "

Would I could think so ! Then, indeed, were hope
To suffer by the loving hand of God.
But no ! I pay no penalty for sins
Deep-dyed although they be. The ills I bear
Are natural—the common lot of those
Who strive and tail. the every day routine
Of Nature, cutting down the barren trees.

"Then, after all, this search for God appears
A kind of fortune-hunting?" Yes ! 'tis so
(For Providence should certainly provide)
But Fortune is not limited to gifts
Of outward seeming. Impulses there are
Themselves a fortune ; such the quenchless thirst
For Knowledge, the idolatry of Art,
The fellowship of Man. the love of God.
—What am I saying? Well ! I thought so once.
And were I but fulfilled with one of these,
My disappointment scarce were worth a sigh.
But here the law of Nature intervenes,
Survival of the strongest ; for, alas.
Like living forms, my thoughts contend for life,
And one by one the luxuries of Mind,
Love of the Wise, the Beautiful, the Good,
Have in their turn succumbed to love of Self
Which now pervades my being. Thus at last,
Bereft of all the dreams that make life dear,
Like to a dying man when all has passed

Save the last instinct, how to draw the breath,
I linger on, a hopeless, dying soul.

But yet one earthly bond remains : my son,
Strangely misnamed ; ' Infelix ' must he be,
Though wherefore thus forestall the evil time
Impending all too soon ?   No ! to myself
I keep my sorrows, giving him my smiles,
That ever he may deem unselfish love
The attribute of ' Father ' here on earth,
A broken reflex in the waves of time
Of the eternal vision, lost to me.
Hark ! striking six ! the boys are out of school ;
I'll to the playground ; thence along the shore
Together we will wend our homeward way ;
Ye gloomy thoughts, be banished for to-day.

> [*Exit* WALTER.

Enter FELIX.

  Fel. Father, good news ! as I was leaving school
A sailor brought me this.   He said it came
From Peter just returned from trawling—"glass
Needing great care."   He seemed himself afraid
To touch it.   What, no answer !   No one in ?

> [*Places a small box on the writing-desk.*

Well, here I'll leave it safe from awkward hands.
Now, for a game at hockey on the sands. [*Exit* FELIX.

WALTER *and* ERIC.

Wal. This evening then, shall test your new defence
In the Queen's gambit?
   Eric.   Not to-night, my friend;
Impressions ever fleeting must be seized
Betimes.
   Wal.   The Magnum Opus has a claim
Prior, no doubt, to pleasure. Still—
   Eric.   To dreams
I know thee ever gentle, and a dream
My work perforce must seem, to those who flout
At metaphysics as a hopeless quest,
The 'north-west passage' of the Intellect.
   Wal. Nay! though explorers find no channel free,
Their labour is not lost. How many lives
Lie misadventured on the sunken reefs
Which thou wilt figure on the chart, though Fate
Deny, that following the drift of thought
Thou find safe haven in another world.
But why this sudden press?
   Eric.   As yesternight
I mused, an open book upon my knee:
(An ancient dissertation on the soul
That animates the world) and whilst I watched

The mystic wreaths of pale blue smoke ascend
In vortices suggesting subtle modes
Of force and motion, through my brain there flashed
A sudden intuition of the terms
Marking the process of development
From Matter to Intelligence.   A dream
Perchance, an idle fancy born in smoke,
And scarcely less fantastic in its form.

  Wal. Fantastic are my own imaginings ;
But phantoms though they be, like vampires grim,
They drain my very life-blood.   Prithee, tell
Thy dream, if only to divert my thoughts.

  Eric. No author needs to be entreated twice.
My fancy this—
                        In things inanimate,
The 'individual' and 'circumstance'
Meet on the terms of absolute exchange,
Each giving back as much as it receives.
Each may become the other ; each by each
Is perfectly conditioned ; naught remains
When both have played their parts, save some new
          phase
Of combination.   But in living forms
Even the simplest 'individuals'
Are not conditioned to their full extent.
But trading with their 'circumstance,' retain

Some benefit, since though they take their due
They pay not back its full equivalent.
And this first surplus marks the primal step
In evolution through organic life.
Succeeding steps are questions of degree ;
What use the 'individual' will make
Of vantage hardly won from ' circumstance,'
Freeing himself by subtle artifice
From touch of his surroundings, loosing bonds
Of strict condition. At the first his gains
Barely suffice for reproductive force ;
But in the next gradations, store is made
Enough to form the nucleus of ' self,'
Seeking security by wise device.
So Feeling, in the lowest forms of life ;
Sensation, when the functions play their part ;
Impression, as the brain acquires control ;
Thought, when the mind is free to use its strength ;
All these are interposing barriers
Which check the onset of external force,
While ' self' the strong man armed, who sits within
Cares nothing for the angry roar without.
Indeed so little does man feel the stress
Of outward nature, that he claims Free Will ;
An empty vaunt, for though the bonds be loosed
They are not broken, though they be of gold
They still are fetters, though the walls be strong
Sooner or later their innate defect

Shall manifest itself, no single stone
Still standing on another.   Then the foe
The outward ' circumstance ' shall press within,
And ' self ' lie prostrate, of his goods despoiled.

Is this the last development of mind?
Not so ! methinks that Nature goes too far
In making Life, or else not far enough
In making Death.   The problem ends not here ;
For, walls once circled round organic life,
A lighter task it seems, to make these walls
A living barrier ; to crown the ' self '
A King surrounded by a faithful race
Of subjects, forming up the death-made gaps,
Ever replenishing a fruitful land.
Communities of living forms predict
The perfect body of the higher mind ;
And this my work, by patient quest to trace
The Soul which these societies foretell.
No light endeavour.   Dost thou wish me well?

    Wal. My friend ! if ever it should be my lot
To converse hold with spirits ; then thy thoughts
Shall govern mine, and nothing will I seek
Of ghostly apparitions.   No ! my goal
Kosmos shall be, the World's pervading Soul.
                          [*Exeunt ambo.*

SCENE III.—*A playground. Boys playing prisoners' base.*

Enter WALTER.

Wal. My time is overstay'd ; an evil sign
That talk of Kosmos loses me my son,
Leaving me lonelier for yonder throng.
How merrily that little fellow scuds !
But over venturesome ; and see, at last
He meets his fate, and, captive, takes his place
In prison. Will his comrades rescue him ?
Now is the moment ; ere the bigger boys,
Their enemies, can get them back to bounds.
Why hesitate ? How like to grown-up men
Are children ! these should politicians be.
For, see, instead of playing out the game
They squabble with each other till they lose
Their opportunity. Stay ! there one starts.
Will he be challenged ? Yes ; the swiftest boy
Darts forward, following at speed,
And quickly gains advantage. Which will win ?
How far the little prisoner extends
His eager hand, and stretches towards his friend !
Rescued at last ? No ; ere the two can touch,
The enemy comes up, the comrade swerves,
And, turning, leaves the captive to his fate.
Too late !

        Ah ! woe is me for all the flood

Of memory that surges through my brain
As thought recalls the presage of those words
"Too late!"   Alone, and in a far-off land,
I see the Hero, resolute and calm,
Fulfilled with the great purpose self-imposed
Of loosening the bonds which lust of gain
Unchecked, imposes on a weaker race.
There bides he, watching for the timely aid
That Providence, he fondly trusts, will grant
By human agency.   Through long delays
For grave deliberation, and debates
Political, imprisoned though he be,
He stands undaunted, stretching forth his hand
For succour.   Now at last a Nation's heart
Pulses responsive, and the rhythmic beat
Of custom quickens, till the bonds of state,
High policy, economy, repute,
All, all are flung aside, and naught is heard
Save the one cry of "Rescue!"   Blood and gold
.Shall flow like water.   Once again the roll
Of Fame shall be emblazoned with the arms
Of mighty captains, and another leaf
Be added to the scroll, by mortal hand
Unwritten, and by mortal eye unread,
That of the unrecorded brave, for whom
Is no distinction.   Comes an hour at last,
When all the land is ringing with glad sound.
"The foe is vanquished! nothing now to fear!

Only another day, and then——" That day
Never knew breaking, save of breaking hearts.
Deliverer and captive never joined
Their hands. "Too late!" it was the hand of Death
That clasped the book for all remaining time.

O Type of the forsaken! lives like thine
Are leaven to invigorate the world;
But little liking has the world for those
Who gauge not worth by scientific test,
'Survival by success,' the solid base
Whereon our social fabric firmly rests.
The true antagonist to higher aims
Is Habit; and the great pursuits which shape
Our modes of thought and intercourse with men
Science, and Politics, and Trade, agree
In furnishing a rational excuse
For leaving open questions where response
Depends on terms incapable of proof
By rigid demonstration. These we waive,
Deferring judgment till a future time
Never to come, so busy are our lives.
But yet we cannot so dismiss careers
Adding new chapters to our Book of Days.
We dare not be Agnostics about lives
Of heroes. These we shelve by classing them
Among the ferments; natures which disturb
The body politic, fulfilling thus

Their part, unlike the lot of common men.
We say, " A little leaven may be good,
But not too much," and turn the parable
As recognizing interest our rule,
Unselfishness the foreign element
Good for emergencies ; and these once passed
We gladly seek again the old routine,
Choosing the ' is,' losing the ' might have been.'

END OF ACT I.

ACT II.

DIXI CUSTODIAM.

Scene I.—Room in WALTER'S *house.* FELIX *busy drawing with compasses, etc.*

Enter WALTER.

Wal. Why, Felix, how industrious you are !
I scarcely thought that Euclid had such charms,
At least for you.

Fel.   Father, this is not work ;
I only try to copy, if I can,
The signet of King Solomon.

Wal.   My son,
Intending thus to practise magic arts,
You should not trace the double triangle
(' Pentacle ' is, I think, the proper term)   .
On paper, but on parchment ; nor should ink
Be used, but the more precious fluid, blood.

Fel. Oh, father, you are joking ! But you know
About the signet. Have I drawn it right ?

Wal. Yes, perfectly ; but whence this sudden zeal
For necromancy ?   Much I fear my cat,
The black one, has bewitched you ; but one paw
Is white, and that I think destroys the charm.

   Fel. Well, father, you must know, this afternoon,
Monsieur Girardin gave the upper fourth
A fairy-tale to render into French ;
The story, how a lucky fisherman
Landed a bottle with a leaden seal,
Imprisoning a Genie fast within.
And then he told us how it came to pass
That Solomon—— But do you care to hear ?

   Wal. Assuredly ; though, Felix, you and I
Would manage better than that fisherman !

   Fel. Indeed, we would.   Oh ! father, I forgot,
A sailor met me just when leaving school
And brought a box from Peter.   On your desk
I left it.

   Wal. Thanks !   The boats are fortunate
So soon returning.   Doubtless, Peter sends
A fleet of prizes for my microscope,
Marvels of nature.   But your marvel first.

   Fel. Well, " Solomon," he said, " was once in love
With a Princess more beautiful than day ;
And when he wedded her, she brought a rose
From home, and planted it within the Court
Of Fountains, fencing it with golden bars
In double triangle ; and so she died.

Then Solomon the King was very sad
Mourning her loss, and never smiled again,
And of a crystal jewel which she wore
His signet-ring he made.   Upon one face
A rose was graven ; but reversed, it bore
The sacred name.   The gem was set in gold,
Alike in fashion to the bars which fenced
The living rose.

                Thenceforth King Solomon
Would never from his finger loose the ring.
And every wish he formed was gratified
By Genies, subject to its magic spell,
Until throughout the world the talisman
Gained fame beyond compare ; but ere the King
Had breathed his last, it vanished, nor was seen
Again until the time when Cyrus won
The empire of the world.   Once more it passed
From sight of man until King Philip's son
Discovered it, and so became the Great.
No mortal since has owned it—— "

   Wal.   Not the Great
Napoleon?

   Fel.   Oh! I forgot ; Monsieur,
Shrugging his shoulders, said, " There was no need,
Il était Français."

   Wal.   That was quite enough.
But did your most veracious friend explain
How such a charm so long could stay concealed ?

Fel. Oh yes; "Unless it came by accident
Unsought, 'twas but an ordinary stone."
And that is all the story. How I wish
That I had such a ring! A lamp would do
Almost as well, though.

    Wal.   Quite, if I might say
That it is after nine, and time for bed.

    Fel. Why, so it is. Father, good night.

    Wal.   Good night.

                          [*Exit* FELIX.

    Wal. How long belief in charms retains its strength!
And yet 'tis natural. A rose I wear
To-day, and Fortune smiles. She will not frown
To-morrow, surely, if I wear a rose.
Martyrs have died for logic worse than this,
Bad though it be. But, touching this same ring
Compelling spirits, will our logic hold
By which we argue from experience
Of Mind attached to Matter, that this tie
Is indispensable, and higher state
Of disembodied soul, beyond belief?
Yet, starting from the inorganic base
Devoid of life, and mounting up the stairs
Of life organic to their topmost step,
To Man, we falter, tracing back our path,
Crying, "No further could we pass. 'Twas dark;
The staircase led to nowhere." Just as if
The scale of structure were designed to form

A monument, with Man upon the top !
It seems to me more rational to say,
" Knowing two terms, the first devoid of life,
Organic life the second, we infer
An unknown third—super-organic life."

Nor are there wanting hints that, after all,
The thought so long forgotten may be true
And Earth be animate.   In lifeless forms
The growth by aggregation, and the bent
Of gravitation toward the larger mass,
Leading to nothing save extended size,
Foretold the era of organic life.
The coral reef, the hive, the beaver's dam,
The town, the state, present communities,
The far-off commonwealth of man, predict
A state of being higher than our own,
Super-organic, based on many lives—
The Spirit of the World.

                              I know thee well
Of old, thou clear, cold, keen Intelligence.
I live, and thou regardest not ; I die,
And thou regardest not.   Thou art indeed
The essence of success ; thou takest all
And givest nothing ; thou hast had my life,
But I, poor bankrupt, I have naught in thee.

            *   *   *   *   *

Longing for rest, my restless thoughts press on

As though to cheat the time, until the voice
Of fateful verdict.   Fancies hurry past
Like steeds, first cantering, but breaking soon
From canter into gallop, as of old
While I was still a child, those trumpet-shells
Upon the mantel-shelf would rock when pushed ;
At first with measured beat, more quickly timed
As the vibrations shortened, till they made
A rattle like a railway train at speed.
Why ! well I recollect the night when first
My father brought them home, and started them
To please his youngest son, myself.   But stay :
Not both would clatter, for I call to mind
That one would never answer to the touch
So freely as its fellow.   Which of them,
I wonder, was the sluggard ?   Let me try.
                              [*Tilting first shell.*
That was my playmate.   See ! it still responds.
                              [*Tilting second shell.*
. Ah ! as I thought, this will not oscillate,
Yet both alike they seem ; the shell, perchance,
Is out of balance.   Some unwonted guest
Lodged in the spiral would suffice for this.
If so, my knife inserted thus, will reach
The stranger.   As I thought, an obstacle
Arrests it !   So ! it yields and severed falls
A fragment.   Is it resin ?   See ! it burns
Like some rich aromatic gum, and fills

My room with its sweet perfume. Needs must use
Its parent stock more tenderly. Ah! here
I have it. No! 'tis broken.

                What is this
Fair kernel to the nut of ambergris?
A crystal, set within two triangles,
And graven with a rose?

                It is the Ring!

Say, am I dreaming? Fast the revel speeds
Upon the stately ship. The heavy air
Faints, laden with rich scent of luscious wines,
Spices, and unguents rare; and now the King,
His fever-heat abating, prostrate sinks
In death-like stupor. From his nerveless hand,
Loosened by venal fingers, slips the ring;
Hastily hidden in the softened wax
Of torch propitious and therein embalmed,
Ere she who hid can find, its lot is cast
Among the treasures of the Persian Sea.
In ocean depths for centuries it lies,
Till Fate so wills that to my erring hand,
On which I place it—thus, it come unsought,
Making me Lord of earth, and sea, and sky!

How shall I use thee, mystic gem, whose light
Sparkles upon my finger like a star
Prophetic of the future? Like a king,
Summoning council ere I pass decrees.

The moon, full-orb'd, is mounting to her throne
Above the heights, the sea is satisfied
With tithe of goodly merchandise, and smiles
Placid and calm, in silver vesture lapped,
The wind is hushed, as fits the air of Courts.
My Court I'll hold upon the furthest point
Of yon grey headland jutting out to sea ;
There will I hansel my prosperity.

[Exit WALTER.

SCENE II.—*A headland.   Moonlight.*

Enter WALTER.

Wal. Our lives are spell-bound.   Scarce an hour
         has passed
Since Fancy whispered that my hands were free.
And yet already do I feel the bonds
Fast as before.   No sooner do I dream
Fulfilment of desire within my reach
Than, ere my aspiration takes its wing,
It droops and dies.   How often have I craved
Oblivion, but now the thought betrays
My former ignorance.   Recall the past,
And on life's dial set the shadow back ?
Not so, for that were suicide indeed
If pain be education.   Fool ! to lose
Fruition of my task so hardly learned,

Shifting the bearings of experience,
The central pivot upon which revolves
The golden portal of futurity.
Nay ! if with failure comes the end ; no door
Leading to further possibilities :
Then Nature's law is final, and Success,
Survival of the fittest, reigns supreme.
Why, this the very iron rampart whence
My soul recoiled, and shall I strengthen it
Heaping up earthworks o'er my buried hopes ?
Never ! While life remains, forgetfulness
No blessing proffers, but a curse.

                              Yet life
Might surely make a fairer start from now
With fresh advantage, and the knowledge gained
From past experience ? There was a time
When welcome would have been all help received
From things above, upon, beneath the earth
To further my design.   That time is passed ;
My calling have I lost, and right and wrong
Seem equally divided.   Duty says,
" Physician, thou must save the sickly child,
Though sickly children enervate the race."
His calling binds him.   No such plea is mine,
And therefore the supreme philanthropy
Bidding two cornstalks grow in place of one
To me means only that the fight for life
Is stayed, until the falling price of corn

Raises the birth-rate, when the ceaseless strife
Anew commences.   Nay, no heart have I
For world-reforming.

        Wherefore not request
Advantage for myself—Love, Honour, Fame ?
Ah, no ! not one of these fair crowns I'd wear
By borrowed merit ; they were nothing worth
Unless I won them by myself alone.
Wisdom and Wealth ?

        These in themselves are good,
Well worth the asking ; yet I dare not ask
Unguardedly, for fear they turn to snares.
My idols have they been, not ends to gain,
But influences to propitiate
By sacrifice of life-work at their shrines.
Idols still let them be.   No store be mine
Of riches more than present needs demand ;
Nor more of wisdom than shall speed the quest
To which the recent current of my life
Has drawn my spirit.   To this end I seek
For earnest of the world unseen ; that Mind
(If mind there be to animate this Earth)
Should show itself.

        In yonder little bay,
Scarce larger than an amphitheatre,
The yellow sand. speckled with tiny shells,
Forms fitting stage.   The scene it looks upon
Is Ocean, lighted by the rounded moon,

Now pausing at its zenith, ere it sinks
Towards the sea.

    To this fair strand I turn
My steps, and there, where now the line
Of water slowly yields its place to land,
I will, that by the virtue of this Ring,
The Spirit of the World, in human guise,
Reveal its mystery to mortal eyes.

END **OF** ACT II.

ACT III.

QUARE FREMUERUNT.

WALTER *and* KOSMOS.

Kos. Why am I summoned?   What strange force
  compels
Thought into speech, the ' Ego' of the World
Into the semblance of a mortal form?
I, who possess the keys of human life
And death, success and failure, bliss and woe,
Now hearken to an echo of the past,
A long-forgotten memory that once
Bespoke prosperity, but now forebodes
Evil to my dominion, and I come
To meet with my opponent face to face.
Speak, child of Earth : the charm has wrought thy will.
  Wal. Prince of the World, no war I wage with thee,
Not hostile was the message that I sent,
Nor do I call on thee from idle whim,
Nor yet to prove my fortune ; but to learn,

If learn I may, concerning thine estate,
And if our natures be in aught akin.

    Kos. I hate thee, and would slay thee if I might.

    Wal. Why so? I never wronged thee; nor is
      life

To me so precious; but what stays thine hand
Who claimest sway o'er human life and death?

    Kos. When one who loved me held that guerdon
      fair,

The world could never satisfy his needs;
And all the more I loved the prodigal
Like a fond parent, glad to spoil his child.
But thou who hast the ball beneath thy feet
Askest me naught save questions. Though the World
Be thine, thou dost not worship me, and yet
My strength I may not use nor work my will
Against the wearer of the mystic Ring.

    Wal. Spirit, or what thou art, or good, or ill,
Full little knowest thou my heart of hearts,
Thus saying that I do not worship thee.
Whom worship I besides? How oft one word
Of thine has overborne my Litany,
And drawn me down to earth, a willing slave?

    Kos. 'Tis true, and yet thou dost not worship me.

    Wal. Thou mockest me, else wherefore should I
      dread

The daily search for manna, craving first
Provision certain made for many years?

Should I have crossed the lake, had I not heard
That after service there would be a dole
Of loaves and fishes? nay, hadst thou kept faith
And paid my hire, should I not still be thine?

 Kos. I am not Œdipus, nor art thou Sphinx.

 Wal. How like an oracle that answer was!
I always thought the questioners at shrines
Supplied their own responses.   Let, I pray,
This vain reiteration cease.   Believe
I mean thee well; and if thy portraiture
Be true, and thou the Kosmos, then thy World
Should be the Universe, thy peers the Stars,
And great is my desire to learn of thee
The secret of thy being, if thy life
Has ever known beginning, and the scope
Of thine Intelligence—wilt answer me?

 Kos. Yes, I will search the record of the past,
And read it by the light of after-thought.

  * * * * *

When first I woke to consciousness of Self
I felt that I was traversing the void
With twofold revolution speeding on,
Circling around a nobler form than mine,
Myself encircled by a smaller sphere.
My whole endeavour was to run my course,
Exulting in my own untiring strength;
Nor through the ages has my impulse changed,
Nor ever satiate is my desire

For progress ; neither seek I more than this
Still to maintain the Universal law
Recurring faithful to my place and time.
That law is my delight ; my nature wills
That I unceasingly, with Sun and Moon
Should move in evolutions, marked by man
In change of times and seasons, day and night,
Winter and summer, ocean's flow and ebb,
And larger cycles far beyond thy ken.
But though my circuit round the central sphere
Is shared by nearer and more distant orbs,
Naught know I of my fellows, save the bond
Uniting us.   My life is in myself ;
And all volition and perception turn
Inwards, not outwards.   In this inner life
Sensation plays no part.   There must have been
An age (for it is chronicled on stone,
In characters of fire and frost and flood)
When ebullitions of a pent-up force
Convulsed all Nature : yet I heeded not.
Nor does the course of elemental strife,
Or varied combination change my mood ;
For I am self-contained, and not like thee,
Subject by change to loss or injury.

  Wal. That I can understand, but yet I deem
Such impulse too mechanical for life,
And such sensation too monotonous.
The World might be considered animate

If now and then it wandered from its course.
I might imagine that the Earth could feel,
If ever it were capable of pain.
But in the picture thou hast drawn, I see
No lights, nor colour, only neutral tints,
And little charm has such a life for me.

 Kos. And that which is not pleasing is not true?
But men confuse two processes distinct —
Sensation and perception. Men infer
That perfect Order is mechanical,
Because they know how oft *they* miss their place.
Men think that contrast gives sensation strength
Because *they* find relief in loss of pain.
But tell me, if there were a perfect man,
As soldier, would he ever place his troops
In wrong formation ; or, as sailor, steer
Wide of his course ; or, as a statesman, frame
Bad laws ?

 Wal. (*aside*). (This is a most Socratic shade.)
No, surely, else would skill belie itself.

 Kos. Then grant that I am perfect in my art ;
My nature and my law are one. For me
To deviate would be unnatural.
And pure sensation is not relative ;
The child feels keenly, but at once forgets ;
Men revel in their health and strength and skill
Without contrasting 'then' and 'now.' Nor deem
My life insipid. All delights of sense —

Sweet odours, pleasant taste, melodious sound,
Soft touch, and fairest scene, are tame beside
The rapture of my grand triumphal march
In measured cadence, as I keep my place
Amidst the evolutions of the spheres.

    Wal. Spirit, my speech was foolish ; heed it not.

    Kos. But think not that I prize my outward state,
Rich though it be, compared with that within.
For I recall the time when consciousness
Began to show itself in higher modes
Than those of mere sensation, even whilst
The waste of waters rounded all the land.
Then, where blue seas by sun and wind were kissed,
A cloud-like film of tiny creatures formed,
Free as the wave, and changeful as the breeze ;
And fleeting fancies floated on my deeps,
Transparent inconsistencies as yet,
Till solid ground was formed and blent with sea
Most closely there, where rivers lose themselves
In confluence with ocean, setting free
The springs of adaptation.   Then my dreams
Became coherent, and a strange, strong force,
Less weighty than sensation, though more keen,
Impressed me with the touch of sympathy
For living things that doomed to ceaseless war
For mere existence, strive, nor rest content
With bare success, but make success, advance.
Still, as I watched the ages wax and wane,

Fraught with the future of organic life,
And traced the steps by which Sensation yields
Its birthright to Impression, in myself
Impressions ever strengthened. Thus at length
When Man appeared, and Thought usurped the
    place
Pre-eminent, I saw in human eyes
A multiform reflection of myself,
And knew the genesis of Mind complete.

Wal. I doubt not that Existence, when detached
From gross material bondage, far transcends
In liberty of thought, the lower state
Of liberty of action. To its depths
My soul is stirred ; now therefore, answer me
By what degrees does Intellect arise
From Sense ; and passing on beyond the bounds
Of Mind attached to Matter, does a state
Super-organic, abstract Thought, exist ?

Kos. Thy question I will meet by analogue.
Supposing that we two were born as slaves,
Deprived of all the rights of property,
Should we not find that when our toil was done
No gain whatever would remain to us ?

Wal. That would indeed be so.

Kos.   Then slavery
Defines the hopeless nature of the strife
In things material ; but when we gain
Our freedom, though our earnings be but small,

They are our own, and somewhat we may save.
This the first stand-point of organic life
Whereon the freedman ranks above the slave.
Next, he is independent, and for 'self'
Turns to account whatever fortune brings.
Soon he will be a master, and employ
Servants to work according to his will.
Labour will be divided ; each his task
Will know and do, until at last the head
Devotes itself to management alone.
This marks the utmost limit of the height
To which the nobler animals attain.
But keeping to our analogue (as fits
This age of industry), the race of man
Transcends this limit, for it finds a means
Akin to that which money serves in trade,
Whereby all kinds of things are interchanged
Without their ever passing through the mart.
So Language is the currency of Thought,
Which wanting, though the man might have a mind,
It would lie latent, or so little used
That we should liken his sagacity
To that of elephants or dogs.
   Wal.   But say,
What of the aftergrowth of Speech, whose use
Resolves all times, all places, and all things
Within our own experience ? Ah, books
Must be the paper currency of Thought !

Kos. A truce to jesting, though the shaft strike home;
But note, I pray thee, that one farther step
Is needful ere we reach the perfect Mind.
And here, again, our analogue holds good,
For hitherto the trader has been bound,
Though e'er so lightly, by the exigence
Of his vocation.   Now, suppose his gains
More than sufficient for his utmost needs,
So that, relinquishing to younger hands
The strife for wealth, he may indulge his ease,
Acquiring great estate, and handing down
Both means and inclination to achieve
The highest culture, turned to greatest use.
Then let me paint a picture of the Man
The least of all conditioned by his lot ;
No mushroom life is his ; for noble birth
Links past with present, giving future hope
In the traditions of a lordly race.
The heir to great estate, his revenues
Amply secure, no need for him to strive
For prize of Fortune in the lists of Fame ;
Nor from the point of Mind excels he less,
For large Ambition prompts to princely deeds,
Vast enterprises of renown ; his wealth
Magnificently used, gives outward form
To aims magnificent.
                        Then multiply
By opportunity this great magnificence

A thousand-fold : remove this princely Self
Beyond all chance of failure or reverse :
Crown him with amaranth and asphodel,
With never-ending life and endless youth :
Grant him the grandest aims, the widest scope
Of high Intelligence, until he seem
Worthy of praise, and worship without stint
A very God whose nature is success
And power, and yet again Success and Power,
Then bow before the ' Ego' of the World !

   Wal. I think I understand.   Thy Spirit dwells
As said my teacher, within living walls,
Those walls the great community of Man
But so far all thine inward life is lost
In contemplation.

                  Tell me next, I pray,
How far extends thine active influence ?

   Kos. I live for progress ; all my inward force
Is spent in perfecting the art of life
(Self-preservation wearing two-fold guise
Of Enterprise and Vigilance) in Mind
As Nature strives to perfect it in Form.
Nature is my involuntary life,
And she throughout organic structure prompts
That forms should break beyond their narrow bounds
And issue forth in new developments
Protective or aggressive.

                  This the source

Of all the infinite variety
Of function, as by endless artifice
The hunter captures, or the prey escapes.
Yet not inhérent is the art of life
As constant presence makes it seem to be ;
Free gift it is of Nature, common wealth
Shared among all that draw their life from Earth.
This gift I share with Man, enlarging Mind
By urging it to fresh development.

    Wal. So far I follow thee : but what the plans
Wherein thou takest pleasure, and the means
By which thy purposes are realized?

    Kos. Like chooses like ; and therefore, though my
        sway
Extends o'er Mind in its less perfect forms,
Yet most my rule is manifest in Man ;
And chiefest my delight in those who rise
Above the common level of their race :
Great conquerors and statesmen, kings and lords,
All who achieve success, yea, even those
The milch-cows of the past, who well revenge
Their kind by draining to themselves all store
Of milk and honey from the promised land,
And trample now like bulls of Bashan bold.
Wealth is the modern arbiter of all ;
All have their price, only bid high enough,
And bait the hook aright, and thou shalt catch
Men at thy will, and whoso gets him gold

Strikes at their source Ambition's secret springs.
Ambition is my purpose ; to inspire
Audacity to stretch, and grasp, and hold,
To make a name, a race, a dynasty ;
To build a stately edifice, so vast
That battlement, and spire, and dome shall rise,
And lord it o'er all meaner tenements.
For, as the sunlight smiles on mountain crests,
There lighting first, there ling'ring to the last,
So do I glorify pre-eminence.
And when I see a soul akin to mine,
Bent on success, by high Ambition fired,
Knowing no bounds save those of its own will.
I count it as my vassal, and within
That soul as in a mirror do I gaze
Upon mine own reflection, satisfied
With that fair semblance, worshipping Myself,
And in the darkest night I show the path
To him whose face is turned towards mine own.
And Light is still best emblem for the means
Whereby I urge the crowd to fresh attempts.
Self-preservation needs no outward help,
It comes by Nature, and the creature clasps
The nearest help instinctively by touch ;
But when men act by reason, then they need
External aid to guide them in their choice.
For, as the sight to touch, so reason stands
To instinct : vain were keenest sense of sight

Without the light to see by ; mine that light
Which I bestow at will.   Look forth, and say,
What dost thou see ?

    Wal.   What can I see, beside
The setting moon, strewing the sea with gems,
Right royal pathway, stretching from the verge
Of Ocean to our standpoint ?

    Kos.   On that path
Dost thou mark anything ?

    Wal.   On that bright wake
I see a fishing-boat, whose hull and mast
Stand forth so clear, that every rope and block
Are visible, although so far.

    Kos.   And all
The ships of all the navies in the world,
Lying beyond that track of light, could scarce
Divert thy gaze from yonder cockle-shell,
On which I concentrate my influence.
'Tis thus that I accentuate men's thoughts
Turning them to my will —

    Wal.   One moment's grace.
I ever thought that reasoning was free
The balance of comparison between
Contrasted weights ; the process complex oft,
But still a question of degree, and lo !
Thou callest it an arbitrary point,
Determined by the bias of thy mind,
What, then, is freedom of the Will ?

Kos.   Free choice
Is true enough, apart from thought of ' self : '
I do not care for problems in the air,
And only in so far as choice affects
Advantage personal, am I concerned.
But when Ambition wills, yet does not dare,
I stimulate faint hearts, and by my light
Mole-hills seem mountains, every fancied slight
An injury, each fortune missed a loss,
Tinsel and beads, as gold and priceless gems ;
And so I fire the mind to swift resolve,
And strife for dominance, and urge it on
Regardless of the cost, to victory.

    Wal. One other word : I gather from thy speech,
In that thou sayest that thy light is cast
Sometime without, and sometime with intent,
That not thine own it is.   Judge I aright ?

    Kos. What matters that to thee ?

    Wal.   I charge thee, speak
By virtue of this spell.   [*Shows the Ring.*

    Kos.   I cannot tell ;
But though it be derived from central sphere
Like moonlight from the sun, if not the King,
Vice-gerent am I with unbounded sway.

    Wal. Yet one last word.   Although thy heart is set
Chiefly upon the few, yet all mankind
Is moved in greater or in less degree
By this same influence of thine, to strife

And lust for conquest ?

    Kos.   Yea! and in the days
When men were fewer, as it seems to me
My joys were greater.   Well do I recall
One of my first crude essays in mine art.
Two brothers had contested some small point
Of preference, in which the younger gained.
The elder moodily retired to chafe
Under his disappointment.   He to me
Ever did homage, gauging not his work
By silly notions as to abstract worth
(Which has no being save in foolish brains)
But by the profit which it brought himself.
It needed little help from me to show
How wrong the younger was, encroaching thus
Upon the rights of primogeniture.
But vain the elder's reason, and at length,
Bound to maintain supremacy, he slew
His brother.   Never has my nature thrilled
In fuller unison with trumpet clang
Of triumph, though that call foretold the rise
Or fall of Empires, than with that hoarse shout
Of the lone victor in a desert World !

    Wal. And so of murderers thou wert the first ?

    Kos. Why use that word ?   Not that I care a jot
For terms ; the thing had to be done, 'twas clear
Such a divided house could never stand,
And Nature builds not upon shifting sands.

But trust not that the present age escapes
From charge of murder, though for sword and spear
It substitute the lever or the wheel.
You crowd men out of life as certainly
By taking from their mouths the chance of bread
As if you slew them.   All domains of work
Are over-full, and whoso adds his mite
Of Capital or Labour to the glut,
Supplants some fellow-worker, and curtails
His span of life.   It is not Bread you lack,
But Work wherewith to earn your share of Bread,
And each new birth involves a brother's death.

    Wal. That may be so, but rather would I learn
Of good than evil.

    Kos.   I can do thee good,
And though I love thee not, on certain terms
I may advantage thee.

    Wal.   Then name thy terms.

    Kos. I can do nothing whilst thy talisman
Endues thee with control.   I do not ask
For more than this—that till the break of day
By thy consent thy Ring shall lose its might ;
But I must warn thee, that this word once said,
It cannot be recalled.   Be not afraid ;
I will not harm thee.

    Wal.   Till to-morrow's sun
I will that this my Ring forego its power.

    Kos. What is that flashing in the southern sky ?

Wal. Only a falling star.

Kos.   It is thine own.

Wal. If there were truth in omens, I might ask.
" What of thine ensign ? "   See ! thy Moon has set.

Kos. Where'er I am is light.   Behold thy Ring !

Wal. 'Tis dim and clouded ; all its beauty gone—

Kos. And virtue forfeit, by thine own consent.
Know surely—thou wilt ne'er see sun again
Unless thou do me homage.

Wal.   What ! a snare ?

Kos. Nay ! little need that I lay snares for men
If I but leave them to themselves.   My light
Withdrawn, they dream away their days in schemes
Utopian, with all the facts of life
Softened to fancies.   Then the sleeper wakes
And wearies through the after-years, a drudge ;
Or calls me back, to find an empty house
Garnished with vain regrets for chances lost,
A wilderness of rank destructive aims,
Subversive instincts.   For such growths as these
Mankind may thank themselves.

                              Enough of this,
Thy danger presses.   Truly canst thou say
That thou hast found in me the cynosure
Of Nature, since to me point all her hints
Of any higher life than that of Man.
Say more—my light shall save thee ; by this proof
Of intervening mind, confess me—God.

                                                    E

Wal. What threatens me ?

Kos.   An ill beyond thy ken.
But I can guide thy mental eye to see
Thy peril, by exciting deep distrust,
Intense suspicion, never knowing rest
Until the danger in its lurking place
Stands by my light discovered.   Idle quest
Without my guidance ; for a thousand doors
Stand open to the grave.   A sudden turn
Might snap the thread of life, a careless maid
Burn down thy dwelling, by some slight mischance
Poison be mingled with thy daily bread,
Or murder stalk into thy room ; nay, leave
That hidden weapon, lest perchance the lock
Fail, and destroy thee !

Hal.   For thy warning, thanks.
Be sure that I will watch the livelong night ;
But never will I bow the knee to thee,
Suspicion ! yea, in legends of the past
Well do I wot how ancient heroes scorned
This bait of thine ; they trod the path to death
Fearless, though knowing their impending doom,
But never would they stoop to earn reprieve
By making life a very hell of doubt,
Distrust, suspicion (precious wares, indeed,
For Mind to deal in), turning friends to foes,
Kindred to vipers, and the breath of life
To foul miasma.   Though no hero I,

I am not less than man.   Look to thyself:
Thou boastest immortality ; that boast
Is vain : the dead world by thy side, thy Moon,
Should teach thee better.   Ere thy inner self
Began to live, hers had begun to die.
Soon thou wilt pass thy zenith ; then success
Will turn to failure, each new step a task
For wizards, holding water in a sieve,
Or twisting sand-ropes, till a dying World
To stone thou turnest.   Spirit ! know thy shaft
Has overshot the mark.   It is not death
I dread, but life not fit to welcome death.
And, though this soul of mine be sorely stained
With sin, and unprepared, it ne'er could stand
More ready for its doom, than when it spurns
Thee and thy gifts.   Go ! get thee to thy place !

   Kos. If thou wilt not be guided by my lamp,
In thine own light thou standest.

   Wal.   I have heard
That put another way.

   Kos.   How so ?

   Wal.   Why, thus—
One said, " Get thee behind me, Satan."

   Kos.   Fool !

END OF ACT III.

ACT IV.

QUI TOLLIS.

Scene I.—*The Sea.*

Kos. "A dying World!" Yea! I am waxing old
(These mortals have a knack of putting things)
And well I know the signs of coming age,
Blank spaces in my being, dead alike
To take or give impression. Strange, that Life,
The flood, should cast upon the beach of Time
Discordant natures, foreign to mine own ;
And then, that Death, the ebb which draws the drift
Of all existence seawards to myself,
Should fail to harvest these, and only glean
Their empty shells ! 'Tis then I suffer loss
Irreparable. Is it thus my Foe
Will sap the fulness of my inner life
By degradation, till again I live
Unmindful of the future, and the past,
As in the long ago when living forms
Evolved from matter ? That, indeed, were Death

Once having thought, to lose the gift of Mind ;
To feel, but not to know that I have felt !
A terror seizes me, when I recall
How in the faint grey glimmer of life's dawn
My soul vibrated to an influence
Too deep for sound ; and yet I surely heard
A cry. as of a dying agony ;
But all absorbing was the sweet young life
Of Nature, and I heeded not for joy.

Silent for ever is the voice that thrilled
Across the void, yet now it tells my doom.
How, with Her last faint sigh, the breath of life
Passed from all creatures that drew nurture sweet
From Her fair bosom. leaving barren hills.
Her outward life remains, and joy in sense ;
But never more within will Thought inspire
My gentle Handmaid, who illumines night
With such soft glamour, that Her silver sheen
Outvies the glitter of the golden Sun.

Shall I, too, cry for help, and cry in vain ?
I, who have never helped a failing life :
Why should I ?   Nature to severest proof
Puts all things ; choosing that which stands the test,
The rest rejecting ; and a thousand paths
Lead on to Failure ; to Success but one.
That one alone is 'right,' the many 'wrong.'

Yet in man's jargon 'right,' and 'wrong' convey
Another meaning, and methinks I erred
In giving my Opponent vantage ground
Whereon to plant his ensign. Had I left
Mankind unbiased by intense desire
For mental progress, till misfortune proved
Itself a natural result of life,
The complement of Fortune ; then my sway
Had never known division. But too soon
I pressed the thirst for knowledge ; for, behold !
Its fruit once tasted, truly bitter sweet
Man deemed it, linking to delight unknown
The unknown source of sorrow. Then I saw
A wall of separation rise betwixt
Some part of human nature, and myself.
And o'er that fortress wall there floated free
An ensign not mine own, by whose device
I recognized an Enemy, and knew
That evermore our battle-ground must be
The soul of Man, fair field of destiny.

Two rival standards lord it over Man.
Duty and Interest (the latter mine,
My Foe's the former) claim the right to rule.
Mine was the right : my ensigns wide and far
Floated to breeze of Fortune. By success
The right divine of kings, I held my sway.
What token had mine Enemy ? A dream,

A shadow unsubstantial as a breath.
Then to the proof our hostile claims I urged.
On the unknown my Rival took his stand.
" Thine be it," I exclaimed; " be mine the known.
That narrow streak illumined by the light
Of Knowledge ; all the dreary waste beyond
In outer darkness lying, void of trust,
And peopled by Suspicion."   Soon as said
The unknown world assumed relationship,
Passing for touch of Nature, making kin
To Man, each tree and stone, sun, wind and storm,
All outward forms, and even phantoms born
Of night ; the whole in one Chimera blent,
And animate with purpose preconceived
To punish in the body, acts of mind !
Then Magic ruled, and whoso dared to play
On human nature, on the weak by force,
Or on the strong by artifice, was great ;
Success remaining final test of right,
My standard, to whose emblem man bowed down
And thus I conquered.   Then mine Enemy
Called upon Reason to dispel the mists
Of Superstition, blotting out His claim
Absorbed by Nature.   But again His right
I challenged.   Not for me a middle course,
Or all, or none ; when Animism loosed
Its hold on man, by Reason overthown,
I cried, " Thou claimest knowledge ; have thy will ! "

Then testing Reason by Ambition's light,
I sought its limits; lo! no bounds it knew,
Spanning the whole horizon with its rays.
Where all before was dark, now all was light,
No trace of phantom world and spirit life :
The unknown island, like Atlantis, lost,
Leaving no place for my Opponent's throne.
Nor care I if with Him I seem to fall,
Mankind no more believing in my life ;
For this my gain. No God but self they see,
And worshipping themselves they worship Me.

Yet, spite of victories, I suffer loss,
My conquests only bring me back mine own,
His triumphs rob me of myself. The end,
Though infinitely distant, still must come,
When tried by my own standard of success
I fail, and lose myself in nothingness.

[*Exit* Kosmos.

Scene **II.**—*The Downs.*

Enter Kosmos.

Kos. I know not if the virtue of his Ring
Compel my steps, or whether new-born fears
And loneliness unnerve me, that I crave
Companionship and converse—human needs.

An evil prophet is this mortal : still,
Whate'er his answer, question him I will.

Enter Walter (*unconscious of* Kosmos' *presence, and
remaining so to the end*).

　Wal. I cannot bring myself to think of Death
And Judgment, but my fancy idly strays
To Kosmos, and the bond uniting us.
For bound we are, though this kaleidoscope
Of coloured patchwork, talismanic spell
And Spirit presence, be an empty dream
Born of my own imagining, no sign
Remaining, save this worthless piece of glass.
It matters not : though Kosmos never was,
He represents reality.　In him
I see personified a mental force
Acting within myself, yet not myself,
But common to mankind, which shares control
Over my being.　In the slackened tide
Betwixt the ebbing night and flowing day,
The gist of life presents itself unsought,
And stays unbidden : like the voice of Time,
Unheard amidst the whirligig of day,
To sleepless ears its deep recurrent tone
Proclaims a purpose stronger than our own.
　Kos. (*vainly trying to attract* Walter's *attention*).
　　　He sees me not, nor hears me.　Though the
　　spell

Be loosed, it breaks not ; but some foreign force
From access and from insight bars his heart,
Thwarting my influence.   His form and speech
To me are known, unknown are mine to him ;
And fast around him close the toils of Fate,
His need—my help—for ever separate.

Wal. The faculties which Kosmos shares with Man
Are Enterprise and Vigilance, the arms
Wherewith the mind equips itself for war.
These arms he ever strengthens with intent
For more endurance ; and were all mankind
Cast in one mould, such benefit for one
Were good for all.   Yet different are men,
Formed of diversities ; of natures good
Each in itself, of combinations good
Each in its person, but untimely change
Or disproportion alters 'right' to 'wrong.'
Too little Prudence fosters Negligence ;
Too much, Suspicion : harder still to steer
Betwixt Ambition and Indifference.
Ambition and Suspicion are the ends
Which Kosmos prompts to—errors of excess ;
For with the mind he deals as Nature works
On structure, making good defective aims.
And still, although he drives us to extremes,
Inducing ill, perchance he does us wrong
Unwittingly ; for evil might arise

From good, through disproportion of the mind
In man.   By light of nature Kosmos works,
And Nature knows no evil in excess.
She says too much, a wilderness of lies,
Enacted for deception, turns to farce
The tragedy of life; she seeks too much,
Seizing or stealing, as occasion serves;
She loves too much, transported by desire;
She hates too much, and dyes her steps with blood.
And yet, methinks, without this added force,
To force indwelling, every chance defect
Would reproduce itself.   No standing still
Is possible to Nature: move she must,
Forwards or backwards; her excess is right.
But when such impulse is applied to Mind
It overstrains the limits which divide
'Self' from surroundings, and delivers Man
A prey to passion.   Kosmos gives the cue
From Nature, not from Mind, and when he prompts
To self-completion, then he counsels well;
But when he urges us beyond the verge
Where self-restraint is possible, to wastes
Of self-indulgence where we lose ourselves,
He guides us ill.   Yet Kosmos cannot see
The secret of our hearts.   Unknown to him,
Or Nature, is the self-denying force
Of duty—an absurdity in words,
Incapable of proof; for how can Self

Deny itself?   And so cross-aims begin,
Hardest of warfare on uncertain ground.
Conscience is sure, but has no proof to show;
Kosmos can prove, but Kosmos cannot know.

   Kos. Always the same refrain of 'right and
      wrong,'
Or 'good and evil;' yet he speaks me fair,
Although he loves me not—more wise than those
Who call me "tempter," "evil one," forsooth;
As though temptation, putting to the proof,
Were not the function of the craftsman wise
Bent on perfection.   Rightly does he judge
That "duty is absurdity," unknown
To Nature or myself; as if a force,
Acting in certain limits could be good,
Beyond them evil.   Stay! is this so sure?
I run my course around my central sphere,
Unbiased by attractions towards or from,
So equal are they.   Yet, had either strength
To tempt me from my path, then good must turn
To evil.   Well for me that this my course
Is shaped by instinct!   Did I pause to think
Of 'why,' and balance impulses opposed
Attractive and repulsive, then, perplexed
Betwixt two 'wrongs.' I scarce could keep the
      'right.'
Nay, if these mortals, like their World, must move
Within due limits, but, unlike myself,

Must choose their path, though ever I invite
Further extension, then some strong control
Should check this impulse, using me as foil,
Granting me licence to develop Mind,
So far for good ; no farther, lest it turn
To evil.   Yea ! and even in my life,
In Nature, are there not communities
United by self-sacrifice?   'Tis strange
That these should lie so lowly in the scale
Of structure, that I leave them to themselves !
Is this the reason why so well they thrive ?
Pshaw ! I am doting.   These are Nature's works —
Insects, not men—and men degrade themselves
Copying Nature !   Animals survive
By adaptation of themselves, but Mind
Adapts its own surroundings to itself,
Bent upon Empire.   Evil days, forsooth !
With falling, not with rising Empire fraught.
If men should shift their standpoint of success
From Dominance to Tolerance ; if rest
From strife were all that self-indulgence sought,
Not mastery ; if Kosmos once began
To mould mankind to Fate, not Fate to Man.
    Wal. If self-indulgence, through our own defect
Or Kosmos' urging, make the sum of wrong,
Then sinfulness lies not in special act,
But in itself, an ill beyond the good,
Abuse of means, contrasted with their use.

And I have sinned, who thought my sins so light,
Mere errors, arrows shot beside the mark,
Aims misdirected, strivings after right,
A similar abandonment of self,
To that which culminates in sacrifice;
And when no retribution came in kind
To wrong committed, thought the wrong condoned—
Made good.   Ah, God! my punishment has come,
Not through my sins, but through my sinfulness.
My mantle of self-righteousness is rent.
I own the justice of my punishment.

[Exeunt ambo.

SCENE III.—*In front of an old Manor-house.   Light
shining through the open window.*

Enter WALTER.

Wal. Where am I?   I have wandered for an age,
The burning characters before mine eyes,
"And after death the judgment."   Welcome light!
Token of man's companionship : not yet
Has the last word been spoken, strong **to bind**
My soul to death, or loosen it to life
Eternal.   Who beside myself keeps watch?
Surely some poor unfortunate, whose heart
Seeks solace from the night and loneliness.

[Music from within.

Ah! now I know: only a master's hand
Could render thus the world-familiar theme
Of human claim on love and death Divine.
The Miserere sobs itself to sleep,
Lost in the Agnus, cradled with caress
By gentle fingers, light and tender touch
Of new-born sorrow, soothing it to rest. [*Music ceases.*
No new-born sorrow his: for half a life
Has passed away since Fortune crowned his cup
With best of blessings, wife and children fair.
Then stricken with the fever blast, they slept,
But he awoke to find himself alone.
There, in the shadow of the dim-lit hall,
I see him now, a pensive grey-haired man,
With figure slightly stooping, less from age
Than thoughts despondent. With his fellow-men
Small converse holds he, save when trouble comes,
Or children pull his heart-strings—all his life
Passes in music. When his trembling hands
Rest on the key-board, youth and hope return,
Renewing kinship with his sacred dead.
Will he not play again? He seems to seek
Some treasure; now he finds it; 'tis a song—
No! for he leaves the organ, coming forth
To woo the stars. Though stars their aid deny,
He shall at least have human sympathy.

Enter KOSMOS.

The Musician.

 I had passed through the vale **of tears,**
 And had looked on Death in **his might,**
When **a vision** came to my aching eyes,
 In the stillest hour of the night.

 Away to the shadowless courts,
 My soul from its prison had flown,
And I saw, as they see, who arise from the dead,
 The Presence of One **on** the throne.

 Man might not gaze on that face,
 Like the sheen of a sun-lit sea,
But the faces of all I had loved on earth,
 Glanced back from its depths upon me.

 Like the shiver of aspen leaves,
 In the breath which the south wind brings,
Comes the ceaseless stir of Infinity,
 To the throne of the King of Kings.

 And the tidings brought from the Worlds,
 Are woven together in song,
As the onward course of the Universe
 Is hymned by the angel-throng.

A song of endless design,
Of infinite care over all,
Of a Hand from whose grasp there is no escape,
As either too great or too small.

The fall of a worn-out Sun,
The rise of a System in space,
The birth or death of some transient germ
Too tiny for Science to trace.

No break in the chain without end,
No effort, nor hurry, nor pause :
The present a link between future and past,
The result renewing the cause.

Then my soul sank under the weight,
As my eyes with seeing waxed dim,
And my ears grew dull with the ceaseless strain
Of the ever-jubilant hymn.

Who could bear the burden of Earth ?
Yet a single drop from the sea
Were more, compared with the ocean's depths,
Than this Earth to Infinity !

And though every step be advance,
Yet the Spirit of Progress saith,
" I crown success, but to those who fail,
I bring pain and sorrow and death."

Stay ! surely the theme has changed
To a sweet outpouring of sound,
Old memories rising anew from the past,
As springs well up from the ground ?

" Who bearest the weight of the World,"
And I felt no longer alone,
For the face of one who bends over his dead,
Was the face of Him on the throne.

It was but for a lightning's flash ;
It passed like the breath of the wind,
But it told me that all the misfortunes of Earth
Are known to the Infinite Mind.

Yes ! known as we feel them ourselves,
No mere looking on at our strife,
But sorrow and death, from beginnings of Time,
Existing with pleasure and life.

" Who bearest the sins of the World,"
That word, ere its echo was gone,
Had told why his Master's last night with His own
Was more than a life to St. John.

Ah ! if through my fatherly care,
Some creature its being had known ;
Could I comfort myself, and remain content,
To leave it to suffer alone ?

Could I rest for that pitiful cry ?
And surely the Nature Divine
Out fathoms in love as in wisdom and might
    The uttermost measure of mine ?

" Who bearest," "who takest away,"
    Not here did the conflict begin,
But or ever the Worlds there was present with God
    Self-sacrifice offered for sin.

Nor here shall it end.   Not estranged
    We meet, who were parted on earth,
Though wounded and maimed in the battle to death,
    Though failing the promise of birth.

Though our lives be decades of toil,
    Or pass while as children we play,
The soul that survives is the soul at its best,
    If sin has been taken away.

Though never attaining its strength,
    Though worsted and soiled in the fight,
Not the 'is' but the 'might be' is truly the soul
    That enters the Kingdom of Light.

When greeting my loved ones above,
    When I clasp my wife to my breast,
We shall welcome the life that was broken on earth,
    And joy—that its breaking was blest.

Not won by ourselves is that life,
Nor kept save with infinite pain,
As His Spirit for ever unceasingly strives
To guard us from erring again.

Do birds know the way across seas?
'Tis Nature directs them aright.
Could stars track their path through the meaning-
less void
By clearness of reason or sight?

Their Guide is our own.   We shall find
The path in its seeming so dim,
Now 'so easy to miss,' then 'so certain to keep,'
By instinct unerring from Him.

Each thinks that the measureless waste
Before him has never been trod:
We are seeking for truth, but each wearisome step
Is bringing us nearer to God.

Shall we find Him?   The vision had fled,
Dark clouds rolling down from above,
As the wave of regret swept my sorrowful soul
Away from the Infinite Love.

Kos. Have I been blind through all the lapse of
years
In not perceiving that to those who climb

Seeking the summit of a mountain range,
Though lofty rise the crests of lesser heights,
They lead no further, but the weary steps
Must turn descending, taking lower ground,
Lower, yet nearer to the topmost peak?
'Tis thus in Nature; not the highest form
Chief of his clan, most perfect of his race
By special adaptation, marks the course
Of further progress through development.
That track he left to gain his present height,
But from the level whence the upward paths
Diverge, and choice is free, a fresh ascent
Lies open to the higher peaks beyond —
My empire totters.   Must I own defeat?
Defeat in Life; that those whose steps are turned
From toiling towards the summit of success
My standpoint, free themselves for nobler aims?
Defeat in Death; that then the twisted thread
Spun earthwards, proves no vesture, but a shroud,
* The outcome of a lower life, prepared
To shield the spirit ere its wings are formed;
Then to be broken, while the soul escapes,
Bursting the bonds that seemed to make it mine,
Defrauding me of this my lawful prize?
Yet, were the spirit judged by what it 'is,'
Full seldom would its wings be pruned for flight.
Either the web that man has spun in life
Would lack protective strength to shield the soul

Or, having strength, would prove a prison-house.
But for mine Enemy.   He either lends
His strength to weakness, turning ' is ' to ' might,'
Or rends in twain the bond that proves my right.

Wal. Thrice blessed seed of sorrow ! bearing fruit
In words which link the sacrificial act
With its eternal sacrificial thought
That God would not be good, did He not give,
That Love would not be life, did it not lose.
No other proof of God I need than this
That of all natures, one alone I deem
Worthy of worship.   He who gives himself
Freely and gladly, seeking not return ;
Who silently steps in to take the post
Of danger, holding life and fortune cheap ;
He who lays down all pride of social place,
Sharing the common burden ; who forbears
Advantage ; he who dares to turn his back
On arméd treachery ; who throws his cloak
Of virtue o'er another's sin ; whose life
Is one long sacrifice of all the world
Counts worth the winning.   Show me such an one
(Ah ! how unlike the picture Kosmos drew)
And by the measure of his gifts to men
My heart will own how like he is to God
Who giveth all.   Ay ! even though the flesh
Prove false through weakness, though the faith that
      urged

To daring, shrink and leave the soul to drown
Beneath the waves it tempted.   Though no hand
Be stretched to save, and men shall say, "Twice fool ;
First for discarding well-proved rules of life,
And then for seeking to retrace his steps
Too late for safety."   Though the Lord consent
That Kosmos sift the wheat till not a grain
Be left to bear the blessed hope of life
Immortal.   Yea! though hard experience
Whose quest of torture puts ideas to proof
Of stern reality, with rack and screw,
Bidding us own no higher life than self,
Should from this body wring the bitter cry
Of recantation, disavowing God.
But give me respite.   Then, beneath my breath,
This whisper shall be added, "Still He lives."
Nay!   prove Him but a dream.   Then welcome
        dreams
Truer than waking !   Make the word of God
A lie.   Oh ! then for ever let me lie.
Such dreams, such falsehood, make men fit to die '

END OF ACT IV.

ACT V.

IN EXCELSIS.

Scene I.—A room in Walter's *house.*

Enter Walter.

Wal. A letter on my table! from my friend.
What says he? "Only just a hurried line
To tell you that the point on which we touched
This afternoon—the principle of gain
By measured steps surmounting loss, which marks
Organic progress—finds its analogue
In good outliving evil in the soul.
Sooner or later we must come to this:
That in the highest processes of thought,
Evil, though indispensable to good
As loss to gain, shall only be a sign
The 'minus' never realized.   Be this
Emblem of evil, now a bitter pang,
Cruel subtraction, pleasure lost in pain,
Life quenched in death, yet in the far-off time

Evil shall serve its purpose, not in act,
Only as symbol, aiding us to work
Our sum of Knowledge.   Then in memory
Purged of its grossness, 'wrong' shall be a word
Keeping us from the deed ; contrasted thought
Good, evermore, but Evil, less than naught."

Thanks, good Professor ; but my time has passed
For subtleties.   Too soon the cold wan sky
Will crimson with the life-blood of the day,
And by that light I see a cold wan face
With crimson stained, and know it for mine own,
Yet heed not for my strength of present life.
Too swiftly falls the blow : I scarcely feel
That I myself am stricken, looking on
With far-off eyes upon a stranger's fate.
The hand of Death will clutch me ere I shrink
And thought will fail before I learn to think.

Enter KOSMOS.

Down ! Kaiser, down !   What ails the dog to-night ?
They say dumb animals can augur death.
What dreaded presence makes thee fondle close,
Thy huge paws resting on my knee, thine eyes
Fixed and distended, all thy shaggy crest
Bristled with terror ?   Best that we prepare
Our arms.   [*Drawing his revolver.*
          Now, Kaiser, thou and I could give

A good account of any lurking foe
Venturing on **this** muzzle, and thine own.
Yet every nook **and** corner have I searched
Finding no sign of danger. Thou shalt live
To **love another** master, as of old
Thou lived'st to lose a gentler hand than **mine,**
Loved for that memory.   Lie close and still ;
No need to tremble now for coming ill.

                              [*Lays revolver on table.*

My thoughts still linger where my doubts began,
When, in the perfect order of the World,
I found no proof of over-ruling Mind,
Mankind and Nature seeming self-evolved.
For well I know that, were my fate reversed,
Were I to live my life like other men,
My soul would faint for evidence of God
Beyond emotion.   Daily cares demand
Some shield against the wear and tear of facts,
Whose constant fretting wastes away belief
As cliffs are sapped by waters.

     Kos.   Aye ! these facts
Are fatal to your fancies.   When the pulse
Grows feeble **and** the mental impetus
Begins to slacken, then your vaunted faith
In unrealities gives way to sight.
While your delusion lasts you talk like **Gods**
Above **the laws of Nature.**   Fain **to fly,**
Your first adventure brings you down to earth.

The thousand trivialities of life,
Your hopes, your fears, your need of daily bread,
Dispel illusions.   When you solace seek
For bitter memories, devising schemes
Of over-ruling law, to prove your loss
A step towards nobler ends, you look around
And see that everywhere the men who lose
Lose through their own default.   One hint of mine
Lays bare the naked truth : "Mistakes, like yours."
Your hopes are vain, your past has died, the dead
Rise not again, no higher law exists
Than that of Nature proven by success.
She owns no Lord but Me ; the test of facts
Disproves my Rival's claim.
    Wal.   Emotion thrills
The soul like melody with words unsaid,
"Notes unexpressive."   How can music vie
With sound articulate or sight distinct?
Great God! and was it then for this that Love
Was crystallized in words—that men should walk
by sight when faith is weakest—that the call
Incentive should through Holy Writ be linked
To living memories ?
    Kos.   There spake my Foe,
Unmindful that my tongue is free to gloss
His text and turn it to my will.
    Wal.   The World
Is still the same, His word can know no change ;

His day should have some message for our own.
Ah me! what is His message but a cry
Of pity for short-sightedness of men,
The World He made, the World that knew Him
        not.
'Twas then as now, for no abyss of time,
Or past, or future, circumscribes His light.
'Tis now as then, the World that light denies;
So, judging, and so self-condemned—it dies.

   Kos. "Kosmos condemned!" What evil hath he
        done?
Portent of ill! I heard that question once
Met by a clamour like a raging sea
For death. Does He now threaten death to me?
   Hal. But is the World itself for ever lost?
Still open stands the door.
   Kos.   But not for me;
No boon I crave, nor tamely will I yield;
At least not yet. First let Him prove his right
By something more than brute appeal to fear.
How can I change my nature at a word,
I, who have known no change since Thought began?
What should I do—who only love success,
The pomp, the show, the dignity of state,
The glory of achievement—were my aims
No longer vast, but limited by terms
Of weakness like an anxious mother's care
For sickly children? Nay, suppose this change

Effected in myself, the World transformed
By social instincts, all for common good
Working, and raising up the lower forms
By sacrifice of those whom Nature framed
For high position.   Would that level prove
So fair in uniformity of life
As varied landscape, rich in light and shade,
In striking outlines, heights the more sublime
For depths profound.   Or were this possible,
Were happiness secured for all the World,
For all mankind by levelling extremes ;
Would peace continue longer than sufficed
For lower forms to reproduce themselves,
Untrammelled by restraints which higher sense
And farther sight would place upon the wise ?
No ! socialists are priests of anarchy ;
Survival of unfitness taking place
Of natural selection.
(*To* WALTER)   Child of Earth !
Thy very folly proves thy parentage,
More bent upon the future of the World
Than on thine own.   The World can guide itself
Leaving this problem still unsolved to men,
Statesmen, economists, philosophers,
True princes of the Mind.   When these can prove
Their answer by continued happiness
Void of declension, then, but not till then,
Will Kosmos change his Nature.

                              Dark and dread
The night is closing round thee.   Towards the day
Choose thine own path; the World knows not the
       Way.   [*Exeunt ambo.*

Scene II.—Walter's *study.*

Wal. Yes! I am ready, I have looked my last
On Felix, little dreaming in his sleep
Of coming sorrow.   Time enough for dreams
When sorrow cometh.   When the World is full
To overflowing, then will sleep be best.

Why am I always harping on one string,
Or wherefore vex myself about the World;
Save that the World is naught but 'self' writ large,
The same drear facts encompassing like seas
Nature and Human Nature, Earth and Man?
An age there was, when in the seething mass
Of fervid elements, ere land took shape,
No place was found for any living germ.
An age must come, when seas shall be no more,
And cold dull stone enshrine each lifeless form.
Impossible is Life, the source and end
Of personality; its secret springs
Unknown, untraceable, and yet it *is.*
A dark and gloomy sea encircles Man,
The sea of Death that gains the world for self,

Gulfing the promise of eternal life,
The Life which gives and loses all for Love.
Full easily we prove this Love away,
Tracing it backwards to a blind desire,
Or forwards to enlightened selfishness.
Philanthropy is nothing but a name
For outcome of conflicting interests,
Survival of the aims which best ensure
The firmest basis for the social scheme ;
Impossible is Love, and yet it *is.*
So Love, like Life, is borrowed, not possessed,
A passing guest, entreated for a while,
A miracle so contrary to sense
That, looking to the origin of things,
We certainly affirm, " It never was ; "
And, searching through the future, we predict
" It never shall be."   Yet this sojourner,
Haply this angel welcomed unawares,
Whilst present with us, still submits to law,
Bound to the 'possible' whose terms confine
Our small horizon.   Then the spirit frets
Against the iron laws that bar its cage,
Striving to break its chains, though closest ties
To all that makes this earthly mansion fair :
The Letter kills, the Spirit giveth life.

Free is the Spirit ; bind it to the Law,
Proving its presence, holding it in chains,

Like breath it passes. 'That we thought was Love
Was naught but impulse. All that seemed Divine
Was only natural, the cause unknown,
The facts not well reported.' In the World
We see that failure sometimes breeds success,
Turning our steps to more propitious fields ;
' Such failure is but seeming, not in truth ;'
We feel that faith may surer prove than sight ;
'Thus men by night have safely traversed paths
By day impassable for dangers seen ;'
We watch how interweaving of our lives
Represses evil ; 'So it stifles good.'
All this is but the commonplace of life
Fruit of experience, to commonplace
Turning our aspirations.

               Is it true?
True, but misleading ; only half the truth.
Our definitions kill us. Day by day
Foreknowledge of results pollutes the springs
Of living water ; blessings traced to laws
Becoming curses. "Charity foreseen
Serves but to pauperize : our acts of grace
From rich to poor, are taken by the crowd
As sops for Cerberus—our crying wrongs
May cry for ever, till the people rise
Frighting the rich, and thus secure Reform
Through fear of Revolution." This the voice
Of Reason prophesying things to come

From knowledge of the past.   An evil word
She gives the future.

                    Keener grows the fight
For work.   No work for those who fail to bear
Contracted leisure, longer hours of toil,
More scanty wages.   Slavery returns
In fact though not in name ; from time to time,
Invention quickened breeds more hopeless glut ;
Thrift becomes penury ; abiding fear
Of aught that checks the loom, the forge, the mine.
Insists on peace, whatever be its shame,
Yet keeps an armèd watch to guard the hive
Whose heaped-up wealth shows greater from the depth
Of poor surroundings.   Terror for the rich
By day, by night ; though swarms of hangers-on
To luxury, perfect the arts of life,
Subverting nature.   For the poor, Desire,
Unchecked by sentiment, enhanced by sense
Of naught to lose, and everything to gain.
The end, though oft delayed, must come at last
Through cruel education, making men
Strong and enduring, fertile in resource,
A hard, exacting, ruthless, selfish World.

Yet try another Fate.   The code of laws
Suppose completed, perfect in its scheme
Of endless detail, warding off extremes,
Seeking equality, restricting press
Of competition, giving each his share

Of bread, and work, and leisure, making Earth
The paradise of labour—still there comes
A future crowd to make this plenty, need :
Till checked by arts protective, Dead Sea fruits
Of false philosophy, the mean is reached,
The equilibrium of stagnant life,
An idle, weak, yet not less selfish World.

Perish the thought ! our boasted truths are false.
Blind guides to blind conclusions ; past the ken
Of Egoist or Altruist, there lie
The world-wide issues of competing laws,
For he who looks upon the two extremes
The individual and social ends
Whose ups and downs in sequence alternate,
Is looking not on conflict but on force ;
The ups and downs that turn the wheel of life
By balanced contrariety.   'Tis thus
The rule of Kosmos passes : not for one
Who brooks no loss, to know when loss is good
For him who loses as for him who gains.
Yet, blind and grasping, in his fall he brings
Our temple with him ; where his empire fails
No God shall reign.   He prompts us to exclaim
" The scheme of laws that regulates the World
Is self-adjusting like the motive power
That works our engines ; higher life is none
Than that of Man."

O lying death !   Nor World,
Nor Man is shaped by self-adapting force.
No scheme was ever framed to work itself,
To make, to judge, to substitute its laws.
We need an Arbiter (and some would say
The Son of Man is such a Judge) to choose
The opportunity, to use—so far
The selfish instinct for development,
Promoting Men, no farther lest the proof
Of 'right' be lost in that *we* wish—so far,
In turn, the social instinct making Man
More equal, but no farther lest we lose
The test of 'right' in that which others think.
And on this equipoise of interests
Fixed against evil, free for higher good,
Not unprogressive like its fabled type
Of earth repelling heaven, heaven earth,
Shall rest the future of the perfect World.

                              [*Lamp begins to flicker.*

Is this Utopia impossible—
This miracle, for miracle it needs
To hold by law, yet overrule the law?
No ! for we see that daily in ourselves
We exercise Free-will, despite of proof
That every action has specific cause.
Free-will is nothing short of miracle,
So oft-repeated that we miss its force,
Just as we miss in life, when reproduced,

The primal miracle from whence it springs.
Free-will, like Life, betrays its foreign source,
Denoting personality in Mind,
And, prove or prove it not, the thought will live
That men are persons, and that all which springs
From personality defies the test
Of aught save personal experience.
None other than ourselves can recognize
The love we lost in that we find again.
We only have the signs, the empty tomb,
The heart fulfilled, the password to our souls ;
No other word than this can move the World
To harmonize the rival claims of strength,
And wealth, and skill, nor yet begrudge the needs
Of weakness, want, and ignorance—a work
Transcending reason, possible alone
To sympathy, sweet charm of Love and Loss.
And in this unity of interests,
Co-operation in its widest sense,
Co-ordinated by the common bond
Of duty, not to self, or class, or race,
Not even to mankind, but higher yet,
To Him whose name is Love, the World shall live.

[Lamp burns low.

Then, looking on beyond this world of sense
To that within us, where the human soul
Unaided, battles in a hopeless strife
With twofold possibilities of ill

(Internal weakness and extrinsic force)
A hopeless task, to turn them both to good
Losing, to make our loss a gain to men ;
A thankless lot, to own our loss decreed,
No merit, but misfortune, or mistake.
Yet, finding that we live and love and judge
Though Life, and Love, and Choice be miracles,
We learn to cry, " I cannot, but I will,
God helping." Then His Presence proves itself
As trees are proven, bearing kindly fruit
Impossible to Earth. This fruit is Love ;
And where Love is, though holden be our eyes.
Yet there is God. If that companionship
Once be vouchsafed, no more we walk alone.
Our weight of care is lightened ; we may sleep
Nor fear the morrow ; nay, though Life seem spent
In vain, our wisdom turned to foolishness,
Our justice yielding inequalities, we know
It is but seeming, for Almighty Love
Is Wise and Just.
　　　　　　　And thus we dare to say,
" Impossible are miracles ; that word
Is final." Yea ! henceforth we take our stand
On the 'impossible,' on that which *is*,
Which never was, for men to seal it up
And make a basis for experiment ;
Which never shall be, to become the test
Of certain knowledge by prediction sure,

But ever manifests itself anew,
True, though a thousand proofs proclaim it false;
Life, though it visit us in guise of Death.
The forfeit ' might have been' no longer lost,
But found where all is possible—in GOD.

> [*Lamp goes out.* WALTER, *feeling his way,*
> *pushes against* the forgotten box on his desk.
> *It falls to the ground and explodes, striking*
> *him dead, and shattering the Ring* to *atoms.*

THE END.

TIMÆUS THE ALEXANDRIAN.

A DRAMA IN FOUR ACTS

DRAMATIS PERSONÆ.

———◦———

HYPATIA.
TIMÆUS.
CLEARCHUS.
NICODEMUS, *a Monk.*
PAULUS, *a Freedman.*
Student.
Slave.

INTRODUCTION.

———◦◦———

MANY years ago the author met with an accident which rendered his eyes unserviceable except for the purpose of reading at very short distances, and this misfortune resulted in his substituting the sense of touch for that of sight in the arrangement of his papers. Strangely enough the change of method thus introduced appeared to be an improvement, as it gave him a means of reference to objects which were beneath or behind other things, and which would therefore have been out of place in any arrangement which was dominated by the sense of sight. It was but a step from this extended classification of objects to a similarly extended classification of ideas, and here also the change seemed to be an improvement. For instance, questions of 'right or wrong' and 'good or evil' appear to admit of more than one answer, and these answers often involve a

seeming contradiction. Indeed, the acknowledged
difficulty of arriving at an accurate definition of such
matters points to some confusion of terms, and the
common phenomenon of argument at cross purposes
might be taken literally and not as a mere figurative
expression. The result might be paralleled by the
confusion of ideas which would ensue were we only
in possession of one pair of terms to express the three
different ways in which we move upwards or down-
wards, to right or to left, forwards or backwards.
Mankind has improved upon these purely personal
notions of position, thanks to the three great natural
landmarks supplied by the revolution of the earth, the
course of the magnetic current, and the action of
gravity; and the success of this generalization induced
the author to search for some such mental landmarks
whereby to define divergent lines of thought. While
thus engaged on this quest he observed that certain
turns of expression in the Athanasian Creed admitted
of a geometrical interpretation, suggesting a conscious
comparision between the arrangement of objects and
the order of ideas, and that so rendered they would
serve as a connecting link between the Platonic
hypothesis of three pre-existent principles and
the Christian doctrine of the Trinity. Kingsley's
" Hypatia" suggested the plot of this little drama;

and all that needs to be added by way of explanation is an extract from the "Timæus" which contains the material part of the Platonic argument :

The Timæus, c. 26.

"Such being the case, we must acknowledge that there is an idea which subsists according to sameness, unproduced and not subject to decay; receiving nothing into itself from elsewhere, and itself never entering into any other nature, but invisible and imperceptible by senses, and to be apprehended only by pure intellect; while the second, on the other hand, which is like it, and bears the same name, is perceptible by the senses, the effect of production, ever in motion, coming into being in a certain spot, and then again hastening to decay, being apprehended by opinion united with perception.

"Again, there is a third class of being—that of eternal place; which is never destroyed, but becomes a seat (or receptacle) for everything created, being perceptible of itself without the interference of the senses by a sort of bastard reason, though scarcely to be relied on ; and hence seeing it as in a dream, we assert that every being must necessarily be somewhere, and in a certain place, and that nothing can exist which is neither on earth, or in the heavens. . . ."

c. 27.

" This, then, is a summary of my opinion—that there are three distinct things which existed before the formation of the universe, *Being, Place*, and *Generation.* . . ."

TIMÆUS THE ALEXANDRIAN.

ALEXANDRIA. A.D. 415.

ACT I

MORNING.— *The Museum*

HYPATIA, TIMÆUS, CLEARCHUS.

Tim. (to HYPATIA).   You may remember how,
     while ago,
You likened the philosopher to one
Lost in the mountains far away from home ;
That home you said was Virtue, and the paths
Leading thereto were many, but of these
Three were the surest—Justice, Wisdom, Love ;
And he does well who follows one of these,
But whoso wanders from the way does ill.
Yet these three tendencies seem oft to cross.
And good to lead to evil.   Thus I ask
If one, whose sense of right and wrong is blurred

By circumstance and prejudice, may find
Some landmarks to direct his doubtful steps
As though some trusty guide should say, " The track
Of Justice leaves Olympus on the left,
But that of Wisdom leaves it on the right ? "

Hyp. What says Clearchus ?

Cle.   I should answer thus :
Such landmarks may be found; but ' left and right '
Depend on our position. What is right
To him who comes, is left to him who goes ;
So I should need some surer guides than these,
Some outlines of the land through which I fared,
Taking my bearings both by length and breadth.

Tim. Most excellent ; but pray consider now.
Suppose the journey long and difficult,
Through distant lands, as such a search must be
As this for Virtue ; then would ' length and breadth '
Be common terms which all would understand ?

Cle. Nay, then I'd take Apollo for my guide,
And steer by east and west, or north and south.

Tim. And always so ?

Cle.   Yes, would not you ?

Tim.   Perchance.
What says Hypatia ? She, not we, should speak.

Hyp. Thoughts limited by things are incomplete,
And larger views demand extended terms.
Thus definitions such as ' right and left,'
· Backwards and forwards,' whose uncertain sense

Is what each man interprets for himself,
Give place to 'east and west,' or 'north and south';
Words which would be but meaningless
Applied to universal sphere on sphere
Beyond their compass; yet we surely know,
That all essential difference endures
Eternal, after as before the worlds—
So all the folly, and the hate and crime
Which come from our confusion of ideas,
Calling that 'just' which brings reward to us,
That 'wise' with which our own opinion fits,
That 'love' which thralls us though against our will,
These false shall fail, but Virtue still endure
Eternal fount of Justice, Wisdom, Love.

You ask for landmarks—these would but mislead;
That ancestor whose name Timæus bears
Knew the essentials to be self-revealed
Through forms of Being, Generation, Place.
The first is apprehended by the mind—
'Being' conditioned by itself alone,
Neither produced nor liable to change,
Itself receiving nothing from without
Nor into other nature entering.
We know not why it is, nor whence it comes,
But recognize it by its changelessness.
So Justice changes not; yet wherefore law
Is fixed, and certain deeds receive reward

A different idea our senses give
Of Being as a state of ceaseless change,
Ever in motion, springing into life,
Scarce at its fulness ere decay begins,
Then fleeting out of life, a flow and ebb
Alternate—relative to the idea
Of changeless Being which it traverses,
As son to father, form derived from form,
Present ere fashioned, freed to live or die,
Leaving the life through which it passed unchanged.
So Love no satisfaction knows nor rest,
With strong swift impulse working out desire,
Of Generation both the source and end.

But from this meeting of existences,
Being and Generation, so unlike
Yet so alike, perceived by mind and sense,
A third distinction, that of Place, appears ;
For things at rest are ever at their goal,
And things in motion never reach their end ;
So neither rest, nor change, can by itself
Suggest a separate idea of Place.
But when we see that things are sometimes fixed
And sometimes movable, we get a clue
To the idea of Place, which, whether full

Or empty, still remains the mould wherein
Created things are formed, in which they rest,
Or if estranged, the home to which they tend ;
And in this liberty of rest and change
The third existence manifests itself—
Fitness of place, the Order of the World.
So watchful Wisdom, calm upon the height
Her vantage ground, surveys the rival powers,
Custom and Innovation, rest and change,
Till by comparison of old and new
Knowledge is perfect through experience.
Thus Virtue reigns supreme o'er human life,
When Law guides selfishness with curb and spur,
When Beauty step by step leads on desire
To thirst for noble deeds and deathless fame,
Nor leaves that life in contradictions lost
Betwixt the claims of Duty and of Love,
When Wisdom, with divining spirit, marks
How the cross-threads of fate are not opposed
But interwoven, forming warp and woof
Of circumstance—the garment, not the man.

   Cle. One word. You say that Virtue reigns supreme.
But of these rulers—Justice, Wisdom, Love—
Has any the pre-eminence ?

   Hyp.   Not one ;
For surely these outweigh all else, and hold
Co-equal empire in the perfect mind.
And since our estimate of Virtue leans

(Our reason only halting at its best)
Upon opinion, and we praise the good,
Giving it glory, calling evil shame,
And wonder at the largeness of its scope
Compared with mean and transitory ends,
So Wisdom, Love, and Justice share alike
Its glory and eternal majesty.

Enter throng of Students.

To-morrow, friends, we will pursue this theme.
    Stu. (aside). To-morrow never comes !
    Slave (aside).   Ill-omened words !

END OF ACT I.

ACT II.

Afternoon.—Room in the house of TIMÆUS.

Tim (*reads*). "Long have I wandered from the path
    of truth,
Misled by many ways which promised fair ;
And now I, weary, know not where to turn,
Lost in the 'one' and 'all.'"

                    So many paths !
Agreed ! but surely there are men enough
Each path to follow, till we learn the true
From record of the false.   So many paths !
But surely every path does not diverge
At every step from all the rest.   Why, see !
All ways of men may be reduced to three :
Backwards and forwards, moving up or down,
Turning to right or left.   All other paths
Are intermediate.   Stay ! what is this ?
If by our terms of length and breadth and height
(Things finite and create) we represent
Ideas infinite and uncreate,
And if, as fair Hypatia said to-day,

" Essential difference is self-displayed,"
We need no landmarks, but reduce our terms
To three dimensions, since we surely know
That these exist, related each to each,
As length, and breadth, and height. And further still,
This whole creation only simulates
The uncreate ideal universe
Made manifest to mind, as form to sense ;
So analogues of length, and breadth, and height
Display the nature of ideal form.
Ah ! now I see my way, and for the All
I read the Three ; and thus Xenophanes
Failed to perceive the geometric truth
Foreshadowed in the old Egyptian lore
And dimly seen by philosophic schools
(How nearly fathomed by a woman's wit !)—
" We only realize abstract ideas
Through three dimensions, as we apprehend
The shape of solids from their surfaces."
Now here our wisest teachers missed the mark
By trying to include the perfect good
Under one set of terms instead of three.
For Virtue bears three aspects, each complete
And perfect in itself, yet each by all
Pervaded, and itself pervading all.

First, Justice—she who portions good or ill
With equal hand according to desert,

Making prosperity the guiding power
To conduct.   How can higher aim be set
Than hope of meriting the Victor's Crown?
And yet methinks I see another path
Dividing this of Justice ; heeding not
Rewards nor punishments, the strings which pull
That counterfeit of Virtue, which contends
Not for the Victory, but for the Crown.
And therefore Love, that ecstasy supreme,
Refuses to admit the test of worth
By fortune or misfortune, pressing on
Towards his desire, though good or ill betide.
So failure and success, opposing weights
When Justice holds the scales, have no account
In the award of Love, who gives the prize
To best endeavour.   Yet athwart the paths
Of Justice and of Love, there runs the track
Of Wisdom—she who measures and decides,
Asking not if we win or lose the race,
Nor even how we strive to win the race,
But if the race itself be worth our pains.
Justice and Love are blind, but Wisdom sees,
And who would say, 'This thing is right or wrong,
Must test it by the threefold measurement
Of Justice, Love, and Wisdom ; nor award
The palm to him who wins, if fool or knave,
Nor yet to him who runs a foolish race,
Nor yet to him who knows, but does not act.

So Virtue bears three names, which represent
Distinctive characters, and thus we find
The One in threefold semblance, when we strive
To realize our thoughts.   Ideal Form
Is interchange of three existences,
Types of the three dimensions.   These ideas
Are therefore equal, as the perfect cube
Consists of equal length, and breadth, and height.
And each is like to each : as one, so all
Alike in the ideal character,
Each uncreate, eternal, limitless.
Yet as the perfect cube is only One,
Although consisting of length, breadth, and height,
So as existences these terms are Three,
But as consistence they are One alone,
One limitless, eternal, uncreate.
Or—putting this another way—we raise
The perfect cube from any single power ;
For each is all-potential, and the cube
All length, all breadth, all height ; yet every term
Pervades the rest, or we should have three cubes,
One altogether length, one breadth, one height,
And thus the all-potential is but One.

So Virtue comes from three existences
In combination—Justice, Wisdom, Love.
These, as Hypatia said, co-equal reign
In glory and eternal majesty,

Wisdom and Justice being such as Love.
For these three principles are uncreate
And pre-existing ; nor can bounds be set
To Virtue, whose perfection stills exceeds
Our utmost definition, every term
Serving to mark another starting-point.
Yet, though consisting of three principles,
Its nature is but one ; and since we find
Its principles some common features show,
And some distinctive, then of these the last
Belong to their existence, but the first
To their consistence ; so we own not Three,
But One eternal, boundless, uncreate.
And since each principle pervades the whole
Of Virtue (which must ever be throughout
All-wise, all-generous, all-just) ; so each
Is all-potential, yet they co-exist,
And the all-powerful is One, not Three.

So far, the three dimensions are agreed
In their consistence, which we name the One ;
But yet they show essential difference
In their existence, which we name the All.
And as my namesake said, " This difference
Appears as Being, Generation, Place."
For now of these ideas, of length, breadth, height,
The first we realize is that of ' length,'
                [Drawing a single line on the table.

Conditioned by no power beyond itself,
Being, ungenerate, and made of none—
The sign of Justice—fixed, immutable.
And if I represent ideas by lines,
Whereof the first imagined, that of 'length,'
Represents changeless Being—then I draw

>   [*Drawing a second line intersecting the first at
>   right angles.*

A second thus, and this is so conceived
That in or out of Being it may pass
Without confounding the idea of change,
Which it denotes, with the idea of rest.
So Generation is as 'breadth' to 'length,'
Existence neither made, nor yet create,
Begotten of the first idea alone—
The emblem of a restless longing Love.
But from this meeting of existences
Which form the personal or active plane,
Being and Generation, rest and change,
Rises a third, the Order of the world—
Token of Wisdom—choice of what is best.
And this is neither fashioned nor create,
Nor yet begotten, but the consequence
Proceeding, as the third idea of 'height'
Thus traverses the plane of 'length and breadth;'

>   [*Making as though he drew a third line up-
>   wards, from the point where the two first
>   lines intersected each other.*

And now the three dimensions are complete,
And the essentials self-revealed through forms
Distinct of Being, Generation, Place :
Not as three entities of each idea,
But one existence in three characters.
Yet of these powers, Justice, Wisdom, Love—
As of their analogues, length, height and breadth—
Ideas, not things—no one is first or last,
None more nor less, for there are no degrees
Comparative between them absolute,
Identical, or incompatible.
We know them abstract, as variety ;
We know them in the concrete, unity ;
But find no half-way house between these states
In which existence and consistence meet.
We cannot reconcile the impulses
Of interest and passion, which pervade
The active plane ; nor can we formulate
Thought into action ; often, though we know,
We do not act, or act against our will.
Our minds can only track one thought at once,
Yet here three diverse goals demand our steps.
We either strive for one, and miss the two,
Or make our life an endless compromise,
Acting like puppets—by opinion moved,
Not knowing if to tragedy or farce.
We need some guiding power beyond our own,
AND THEREFORE MORTALS CALL UPON THE GODS.

Is this the lever which Hypatia seeks
Wherewith to move an unregarding world
Back to philosophy and quest of truth?
Or is it but a lever in my hands
To move her love? Ah! foolish that I am
To dream of her! As well might clattering steel
Turn supple, and fall soft in silent folds;
As well might Dian's hounds be turned to hares,
And shivering flee where once they hotly chased,
As fair philosopher submit to love.
Ay! there's the secret. Nature diverse gifts
On man and maid bestows; we chase, they fly;
'Tis ours to win; they win but when they lose.
The more man fights for knowledge or renown,
The louder beats his pulse to Cupid's march.
But, when the woman learns like man to strive,
Nor rests contented with the passive voice,
She loses—nay, *we* lose—the art of Love.
Hypatia, like a man, thinks but of men
As scholars, teachers, rivals, not as men;
While I—am I unsexed that thus I note
Each changing turn and accent of her voice,
Each slightest fashion of her broidered hair,
Each careless look or action, each new fold
Of vesture, every gem on neck or arm?
And but to say the thing she said is sweet!
And but to breathe where she has breathed is life!
And but to touch what she has touched is bliss!

Therefore this wine of which her lips have quaffed—
Thrice happy to have kissed those lips divine !—

> *[Taking a golden phial hung round his neck.*

Is hallowed as libation to the Gods.
It may be I shall never own my love,
It may be I shall die before my time ;
But grant my prayer, Athene !   In that hour
Of death and birth, when life becomes a dream,
And dreams reality, oh ! may my face
From this be sprinkled, and my last deep thirst
From this be quenched ! Great Zeus ! my prayer is
      heard,
For lighting on my casement, lo ! a dove,
Bearing Athene's sign—an olive spray !

END OF ACT II.

ACT III.

Enter NICODEMUS.

Nic. Forty years' sojourn in the wilderness,
And Canaan still denied, though every word
Of Athanasius I have straitly kept.
" I leave my work unfinished—thine the task
To find the chosen servant of the Lord,
Ordained to crown the edifice of faith."
These his last words—as he with trembling hands
Placed in my grasp the scroll whereon is writ
The marvel of Three Persons and One God.
Henceforth I knew no rest, but ever sought
From holy men for oracles divine
To make the symbol perfect.   All in vain—
For some said " nought was wanting in the stream,
Full to overflowing, bright and clear as day ; "
Others, " that so sublime a mystery
Passed human knowledge, and must aye be hid."
And in this questioning my life is spent,

So that I fain must yield my precious charge,
Like the one talent, neither more nor less
Than when bestowed.   Here let me pass the night ;
To-morrow I will render up the scroll
To Bishop Cyril ; then await my doom,
Unprofitable servant that I am.

Enter Paulus.

Pau. A priest ! the Lord be praised !
Nic.   Amen !
Pau. Father, a dying man requires thy prayers
And the last offices of Holy Church.
Nic. I come, my son.
Pau.   Not even asking where ?
Nic. Man cannot answer that which I would ask.
Pau. (*aside*).   These anchorites are all a little mad.
(*To* Nicodemus). And yet my story you should hear.
Nic.   Say on
Pau. Well, then.   This afternoon I heard a shout,
And running out, I saw a frantic crowd
Surging like waves across the Julian Way ;
And shrill above the din went up the cry,
" Death to the witch, tear her from limb to limb !"
And for one moment o'er the sea of heads
Rose a white face, then sank no more to rise ;
And so the mob pressed on, and so to death
Hypatia passed.
Nic. Hypatia ! Who was she ?

Pau. Why, she bewitched the city with her arts,
And justly met her doom.   Well, as I turned
Homeward again, I saw upon the path
A helpless figure lying, hurt to death
By trampling feet ; and then a woman cried
From out a window—she had seen him strive
To snatch Hypatia from the grasp of one
Who bore her on his shoulder ; but he fell
Struck by a dozen hands ; so there he lay.
And I was passing on, when, as in sleep,
He moved, and o'er his face there flushed a smile,
Waking I know not what strange memories
Within my breast ; and so I, stooping, asked,
" Art thou a Christian ? " but he shook his head,
Still smiling ; and I turned away again,
When, with a fluttering sound, a snow-white dove
Hovered above us ; and I knew the sign,
And questioned thus : These women are such fools !
Perchance he only strove to be the first
To offer up the sacrifice ; perchance
He meant—" not yet a Christian "—since the rite
Baptismal he as catechumen lacked ?
And looking upward at the blessed dove,
I saw that I had guessed—for in its beak
It bore an olive branch, whereby I knew
That it prefigured the salvation great
Of water to our second father given.
And so the wounded man I carried home,

And laid him on my bed, and tended him ;
And evermore I blessed the guiding dove
That one so holy was not left to die
An outcast ; for his fingers never ceased
To trace the sacred sign of Him who died
For sinful men ; and ever in his speech
He called upon the blessed Trinity with words
Of mystic import.   Nay ! no need for haste,
The door is here.

   Nic.   Quick ! quick ! when once the door
Is shut, the foolish ones may knock in vain !

                        [They enter hurriedly.

END OF ACT III.

ACT IV.

SUNRISE.—*Room in the house of* PAULUS.   NICODEMUS
near table with writing-materials.   TIMÆUS *on a couch.*

Nic. Yet I had hoped ; prophetic seemed the sign ;
But not for me.   [*Rising and looking at* TIMÆUS.
                    Poor boy ! for such thou art
Beside my weight of years ; what couldst thou teach
Of the great mystery from angels hid?
            [*Sits down and takes from his bosom a scroll.*
This my last look upon these hallowed words
Which other hands shall claim.   How firmly traced
This sentence which maintains the deity
Of Father, Son, and Spirit—" Persons Three
Whom man may not confound, but Substance One
Which man may not divide, Whose glory shines
Equal in co-eternal majesty."
Here the pen falters, as though faint and spent
In soaring through the infinite abyss ;
And oft I long for chosen words to tell
Wherein the nature of these glories Three,

Seeming so different, is Unity,
And thus maintain the first and greatest law,
That God is One.   Yet, were this gift vouchsafed,
I fear to fall into idolatry
For want of some sure test beyond the sense,
Lest I should bow before the outward signs
Of majesty, for majesty itself—
Lost in the glories which Thy presence sheds.

The glory of the Father—King of kings,
And Judge of all men, seated on His throne,
Surrounded by the countless hosts of heaven,
Holding His court of Justice on mankind,
The glory of the Son—who left His throne
Because all majesty was nought to Him
While yet one sheep was missing from the fold :
And so among us came incarnate Love—
Not that we loved Him, but that He loved us—
And triumphed, taking manhood into God.
And so the glory of the crown of thorns
Equals the glory of the crown of gold ;
And youths and maidens hesitate to choose
Whether to serve their God within His courts,
Making their life acceptable to Him,
Or going forth into this sinful world,
Losing themselves to win back other lives.
And so with heavy heart and languid pulse
Some start in contest for the golden crown,

I

While others, joyful and with nimble feet,
Follow the path whose ending is the cross.
Most Holy Spirit! be Thy glory mine,
Who can no crown achieve, but only wait,
Like handmaid on her mistress, for the voice
Of Wisdom, making wise my foolishness.
No crown Thou wearest, but Thy glory lies
In peace and stillness, which no worlds can give
Nor take away.   O'er chaos thou didst breathe,
And order was.   Thy voice the Tishbite heard,
Quiet and small, and lo! the ways Divine,
By law and zeal obscured, were manifest.
Whilst in our pride of reason and of strength
We question Justice as too hard a law,
We question Love as contrary to law,
Then comes the quiet of the frame bowed down
By sickness, and in watches of the night
That formless presence floats before our eyes,
That whisper penetrates our heart of hearts—
"A father's justice always ends in love,
A father's love can never be unjust."

Thus Wisdom with divining spirit speaks,
And lo! a glory fills the listening soul,
Gift of the Spirit, not as fits a king,
Nor like to that of martyrdom, but sweet
As the hushed calm which overspread the lake
When the command was given, "Peace, be still!"

Tim. "Father and Son!"—the very terms *she* used
For the relation Justice bears to Love.
"Divining Spirit!" these *her* self-same words,
For Wisdom judging betwixt rival claims,
Father, Son, Spirit—I accept the terms
For Justice, Love and Wisdom; and again
I work my problem of the afternoon,
Defining how these characters exist
In one consistence, as length, breadth and height
In threefold semblance. Equally they share
Glory and co-eternal Majesty.

Nic. Why, so 'tis writ! Surely he does not mock!
Silence, my beating heart—he speaks again!

Tim. Such as the Father, such again the Son,
And such the Spirit.

Nic. (writing).   "Such the Holy Ghost!"
Swift, swift, my pen!

Tim.   The Father uncreate—

Nic. Himself Creator!

Tim.   Uncreate the Son—

Nic. Before all worlds!

Tim.   The Spirit uncreate.
The Father whom no terms can comprehend;
The Son incomprehensible;

Nic.   Amen.

Tim. Incomprehensible the Spirit.

Nic.   Yea!
(*Writing*). "Incomprehensible the Holy Ghost."

Tim. Eternal Father, and eternal Son;
Spirit eternal; yet these are not Three,
Eternal, uncreate, and limitless,
But One, eternal, boundless, uncreate.
Once more.   The Father is omnipotent;
The Son almighty; and all-powerful
The Spirit; yet these are not Three, but One
Omnipotent.

   Nic. (*writing*).   "But One!"   So now the sense
Is clear of this, I find already writ,
That not Three Gods, nor Lords, exist, but One.
And thus we make confession of belief
In Unity—but still there lacks the proof
Of Trinity.

   Tim. ,   The Father made of none,
Neither create, nor generate.   The Son——

   Nic. (*writing*).   "The Son!"   Oh! wherefore dost
        thou pause, dear youth?
And why with trembling fingers dost thou trace
A line upon thy breast?

   Tim.   The Father thus—
                  [*Making first sign.*

   Nic. And cross it by another line?

   Tim.   The Son——
                  [*Making second sign.*

   Nic. Oh! blessed Jesu!   Is it by the cross
Alone, that with the Father thou art seen?

   Tim. Is only of the Father, not create

Nor made, but generate.   The Spirit——

   Nic.   Aye!

(*Writing*): "The Holy Ghost!"   What means he by
      that sign,

As though he drew the life-blood from his heart?

   Tim. Not made, create, nor generate, but thus

Proceeding.   [*Making* **third** *sign.*

          So the Father, One, not Three—

One Son, and not Three Sons—the Spirit One,

Not Three—and in this Trinity nor first

Nor last is known, none greater and none less.

   Nic. (*writing*). "None less!"   My task is done, for
      here 'tis writ

That so co-equal are the blessed Three,

And co-eternal.   Glory be to God!   .

             [*Rising and going to the bedside.*

Poor boy!   He sleeps, and ever in his dream

He sees the holy angels, for he smiles.

Surely he passeth out of death to life,

A spotless soul, unsullied by the world,

Yet unbaptized.   Stay, what is this that shines

Fair on his breast?

          [*Taking the phial from* Timæus' *neck.*

         Why, this is precious wine!

Some relic doubtless of a sacred feast

Prepared for men devout and virgins pure,

From whom he learned these holy mysteries;

Nay! for he said, "*her* words"—perchance *she* stands

Before her Lord, her maiden robe of white
Becrimsoned with the blood of martyrdom.
Water is wanting, but the bridal Guest
Of Cana surely will vouchsafe to bless
This for the needful rite

> [*Sprinkling the face of* TIMÆUS.

                              I thee baptize
As Athanasius, bearing thus the cross   [*Making sign.*
In name of Father, Son, and Holy Ghost !
Still a few drops remain, and I, poor priest,
Yet still a priest, unworthy these to share,
Yet still by grace a witness to the work—
These, in communion with those that sleep,
In memory of death which purchased life,
With thee I thus partake.

> [*Drinks and gives to* TIMÆUS.

   Tim.   No longer Thought,
But Life ! She beckons me ! Her eyes are sad,
But full of love unspeakable ! I come !   [*Dies.*
   Nic. Mother of Jesu ! Blessed be the dead !

THE END.

THE MASTER'S WINDOW.

THE MASTER'S WINDOW.

I missed my train at the station,
    And had several hours to wait :
    So I sauntered through Friars-gate.
And made my way to the Minster,
Where a dear old Quaker spinster
    And a man from Nevada in black,
    Were suffering under the clack
Of the verger's demonstration.

The Westerner polished his hat,
    And stared with inscrutable smile
    Along nave and transept and aisle,
And his atmosphere prosaic
Was so fatal to thoughts archaic
    That the guide's perfunctory lecture,
    With its details of architecture,
Took a chill and fell hopelessly flat.

Yet in one side-chapel we listened
   'Mid the organ's far-off thunder,
   As we stood before a wonder
Of colours broken and dim,
Like echoes of children's hymn,
   Streaming down in a golden haze
   With such light of the olden days,
That the dust took fire and glistened.

All the space around seemed vaster,
   Touched with soft translucent fingers,
   Where the craftsman's spirit lingers
In that pure and mystic dream,
And the gates of heaven seem
   Open with foretaste of sweetness
   From the perfect incompleteness
Of the window of the Master.

" He who wrought in such marvellous fashion
   Had lived to see his name
   Obscured, by the brighter fame
Of the pupil, to whom tradition
Attributes that fine composition— "
   Here the verger signed with his wand
   To a gorgeous window beyond,
In the transept, depicting the Passion.

" 'Tis magnificent, every one owns.
 But from the few fragments remaining,
 Odds and ends of superfluous staining,
The Master this window designed.
The Scholar went out of his mind
 From envy, and leaped from the clerestory ;
 And in proof that this is not a mere story,
See the stain of his blood on the stones ! "

There *was* a red tinge on the floor,
 But the Westerner put on a twang
 Most nasal, and said, " Well, I'll hang
If this suicide isn't a fraud :
For this pavement's the sixth that I've scored,
 Without counting the steps at Versailles,
 Where the showman his customers riles
By passing off stone-mould for gore,

" Though it grows in the States by the acre.
 Mind ! I don't say but what these two chaps
 Might have once had a shindy perhaps,
But at York t'was the young fellow won,
And at Roslin the work that was done
 Was carving not glazing."—The guide
 Took his fee, but in no way replied
As he bowed out the slim lady Quaker.

She—when we had crossed the portal
　　Turned, with gesture deprecating
　　Towards the stranger—hesitating
Blushed, at her own boldness frightened ;
Then a smile her features brightened,
　　And she spoke in accents tender,
　　Soft and still, as those that render
Dying man, to hope immortal.

" Friend ! thy words so lightly spoken
　　Bring to me a gracious message ;
　　That these old-world stories presage
Not the barren facts of history,
But an underlying mystery
　　Of whose presence in our being,
　　To our fathers' child-like seeing,
Yon fair window seemed a token.

" Surely—every noble nature
　　Shapes itself to brightest ending,
　　Through the rich harmonious blending
Of a many-coloured life.
Then victorious in the strife,
　　Like the sun in glory sets,
　　While the gazing world forgets
The Creator in the creature.

" Yet the 'great ones' of the earth
    Hold their state apart from ours.
    Not for us the scattered flowers,
Laurel crown, or cypress wreath.
No! we struggle on to death,
    With our bonds of daily duty
    Little lightened by such beauty
As bedecks *them* from their birth.

" But the Master whom we slight
    Fashions for Himself a witness
    Out of weakness and unfitness;
Human skill and strength refusing
Only wasted fragments choosing,
    And from such poor waifs and strays
    Lo ! a work of perfect praise,
Making all around it bright.

" Ah ! what grace for us, my friends,
    Who in business, or in pleasure,
    Spend our days, save some scant measure,
Scattered fragments here and there,
Snatched perchance, for praise or prayer ;
    That our Master these collecteth ;
    And such harmony perfecteth,
As earth's fairest dream transcends."

She was gone—and the Westerner peered
    Into space, standing solemnly chinking
    The coin in his pockets, and thinking
To the tune of a soft sibillation;
Then his hands by a swift extrication
    He drew from their shelter, and placed
    An arm within mine as in haste
Back again through the doorway he steered.

Saying, " Pard ! I feel mean, you may bet ;
    A child could have raised out the boss ;
    But, *she*—well !   I weaken, old hoss.
Say ! that show must be paid for, I guess."
And the poor-box within the recess
    Was enriched by a handful that rolled
    With the glitter and tinkle of gold—
My heart warms when I think of him yet !

THE END.

A LIST OF

KEGAN PAUL, TRENCH & CO.'S

PUBLICATIONS.

8. 86

1, *Paternoster Square,*
London.

A LIST OF
KEGAN PAUL, TRENCH & CO.'S
PUBLICATIONS.

———— ·· ————

CONTENTS.

————————————

GENERAL LITERATURE.

A. K. H. B.—From a Quiet Place. A Volume of Sermons. Crown 8vo, 5s.

ALEXANDER, William, D.D., Bishop of Derry.—The Great Question, and other Sermons. Crown 8vo, 6s.

ALLEN, Rev. R., M.A.—Abraham : his Life, Times, and Travels, 3800 years ago. Second Edition. Post 8vo, 6s.

ALLIES, T. W., M.A.—Per Crucem ad Lucem. The Result of a Life. 2 vols. Demy 8vo, 25s.

   A Life's Decision. Crown 8vo, 7s. 6d.

AMHERST, Rev. W. J.—The History of Catholic Emancipation and the Progress of the Catholic Church in the British Isles (chiefly in England) from 1771–1820. 2 vols. Demy 8vo, 24s.

AMOS, Professor Sheldon.—The History and Principles of the Civil Law of Rome. An aid to the Study of Scientific and Comparative Jurisprudence. Demy 8vo. 16s.

Ancient and Modern Britons. A Retrospect. 2 vols. Demy 8vo, 24s.

ANDERDON, Rev. W. H.—Evenings with the Saints. Crown 8vo, 5s.

ANDERSON, David.—"Scenes" in the Commons. Crown 8vo, 5s.

ARISTOTLE.—The Nicomachean Ethics of Aristotle. Translated by F. H. Peters, M.A. Second Edition. Crown 8vo, 6s.

ARMSTRONG, Richard A., B.A.—Latter-Day Teachers. Six Lectures. Small crown 8vo, 2s. 6d.

AUBERTIN, J. J.—A Flight to Mexico. With Seven full-page Illustrations and a Railway Map of Mexico. Crown 8vo, 7s. 6d.

Six Months in Cape Colony and Natal. With Illustrations and Map. Crown 8vo, 6s.

BADGER, George Percy, D.C.L.—An English-Arabic Lexicon. In which the equivalent for English Words and Idiomatic Sentences are rendered into literary and colloquial Arabic. Royal 4to, 80s.

BAGEHOT, Walter.—The English Constitution. New and Revised Edition. Crown 8vo, 7s. 6d.

Lombard Street. A Description of the Money Market. Eighth Edition. Crown 8vo, 7s. 6d.

Essays on Parliamentary Reform. Crown 8vo, 5s.

Some Articles on the Depreciation of Silver, and Topics connected with it. Demy 8vo, 5s.

BAGOT, Alan, C.E.—Accidents in Mines: their Causes and Prevention. Crown 8vo, 6s.

The Principles of Colliery Ventilation. Second Edition, greatly enlarged. Crown 8vo, 5s.

The Principles of Civil Engineering as applied to Agriculture and Estate Management. Crown 8vo, 7s. 6d.

BAKER, Sir Sherston, Bart.—The Laws relating to Quarantine. Crown 8vo, 12s. 6d.

BAKER, Thomas.—A Battling Life; chiefly in the Civil Service. An Autobiography, with Fugitive Papers on Subjects of Public Importance. Crown 8vo, 7s. 6d.

BALDWIN, Capt. J. H.—The Large and Small Game of Bengal and the North-Western Provinces of India. With 20 Illustrations. New and Cheaper Edition. Small 4to, 10s. 6d.

BALLIN, Ada S. and F. L.—A Hebrew Grammar. With Exercises selected from the Bible. Crown 8vo, 7s. 6d.

BARCLAY, Edgar.—Mountain Life in Algeria. With numerous Illustrations by Photogravure. Crown 4to, 16s.

BARLOW, James W.—The Ultimatum of Pessimism. An Ethical Study. Demy 8vo, 6s.

Short History of the Normans in South Europe. Demy 8vo, 7s. 6d.

BAUR, *Ferdinand, Dr. Ph.*—A Philological Introduction to Greek and Latin for Students. Translated and adapted from the German, by C. KEGAN PAUL, M.A., and E. D. STONE, M.A. Third Edition. Crown 8vo, 6s.

BAYLY, *Capt. George.*—Sea Life Sixty Years Ago. A Record of Adventures which led up to the Discovery of the Relics of the long-missing Expedition commanded by the Comte de la Perouse. Crown 8vo, 3s. 6d.

BELLASIS, *Edward.*—The Money Jar of Plautus at the Oratory School. An Account of the Recent Representation. With Appendix and 16 Illustrations. Small 4to, sewed, 2s.

The New Terence at Edgbaston. Being Notices of the Performances in 1880 and 1881. With Preface, Notes, and Appendix. Third Issue. Small 4to, 1s. 6d.

BENN, *Alfred W.*—The Greek Philosophers. 2 vols. Demy 8vo, 28s.

Bible Folk-Lore. A Study in Comparative Mythology. Crown 8vo, 10s. 6d.

BIRD, *Charles, F.G.S.*—Higher Education in Germany and England. Being a brief Practical Account of the Organization and Curriculum of the German Higher Schools. With critical Remarks and Suggestions with reference to those of England. Small crown 8vo, 2s. 6d.

FLECKLY, *Henry.* Socrates and the Athenians: An Apology. Crown 8vo, 2s. 6d.

BLOOMFIELD, *The Lady.*—Reminiscences of Court and Diplomatic Life. New and Cheaper Edition. With Frontispiece. Crown 8vo, 6s.

BLUNT, *The Ven. Archdeacon.*—The Divine Patriot, and other Sermons. Preached in Scarborough and in Cannes. New and Cheaper Edition. Crown 8vo, 4s. 6d.

BLUNT, *Wilfrid S.*—The Future of Islam. Crown 8vo, 6s.

Ideas about India. Crown 8vo. Cloth, 6s.

BODDY, *Alexander A.*—To Kairwân the Holy. Scenes in Muhammedan Africa. With Route Map, and Eight Illustrations by A. F. JACASSEY. Crown 8vo, 6s.

BOSANQUET, *Bernard.*—Knowledge and Reality. A Criticism of Mr. F. H. Bradley's "Principles of Logic." Crown 8vo, 9s.

BOUVERIE-PUSEY, *S. E. B.*—Permanence and Evolution. An Inquiry into the Supposed Mutability of Animal Types. Crown 8vo, 5s.

BOWEN, *H. C., M.A.*—Studies in English. For the use of Modern Schools. Eighth Thousand. Small crown 8vo, 1s. 6d.

English Grammar for Beginners. Fcap. 8vo, 1s.

Simple English Poems. English Literature for Junior Classes. In four parts. Parts I., II., and III., 6d. each. Part IV., 1s. Complete, 3s.

BRADLEY, F. H.—The Principles of Logic. Demy 8vo, 16s.

BRIDGETT, Rev. T. E.—History of the Holy Eucharist in Great Britain. 2 vols. Demy 8vo, 18s.

BROOKE, Rev. S. A.—Life and Letters of the Late Rev. F. W. Robertson, M.A. Edited by.

    I. Uniform with Robertson's Sermons. 2 vols. With Steel Portrait. 7s. 6d.
    II. Library Edition. With Portrait. 8vo, 12s.
    III. A Popular Edition. In 1 vol., 8vo, 6s.

    The Fight of Faith. Sermons preached on various occasions. Fifth Edition. Crown 8vo, 7s. 6d.

    The Spirit of the Christian Life. Third Edition. Crown 8vo, 5s.

    Theology in the English Poets.— Cowper, Coleridge, Wordsworth, and Burns. Fifth Edition. Post 8vo, 5s.

    Christ in Modern Life. Sixteenth Edition. Crown 8vo, 5s.

    Sermons. First Series. Thirteenth Edition. Crown 8vo, 5s.

    Sermons. Second Series. Sixth Edition. Crown 8vo, 5s.

BROWN, Rev. J. Baldwin, B.A.—The Higher Life. Its Reality, Experience, and Destiny. Sixth Edition. Crown 8vo, 5s.

    Doctrine of Annihilation in the Light of the Gospel of Love. Five Discourses. Fourth Edition. Crown 8vo, 2s. 6d.

    The Christian Policy of Life. A Book for Young Men of Business. Third Edition. Crown 8vo, 3s. 6d.

BROWN, Horatio F.—Life on the Lagoons. With two Illustrations and Map. Crown 8vo, 6s.

BROWNE, H. L.—Reason and Religious Belief. Crown 8vo, 3s. 6d.

BURDETT, Henry C.—Help in Sickness—Where to Go and What to Do. Crown 8vo, 1s. 6d.

    Helps to Health. The Habitation—The Nursery—The School-room and—The Person. With a Chapter on Pleasure and Health Resorts. Crown 8vo, 1s. 6d.

BURKE, The Late Very Rev. T. N.—His Life. By W. J. Fitz-patrick. 2 vols. With Portrait. Demy 8vo, 30s.

BURTON, Mrs. Richard.—The Inner Life of Syria, Palestine, and the Holy Land. Post 8vo, 6s.

CAPES, J. M.—The Church of the Apostles: an Historical Inquiry. Demy 8vo, 9s.

Carlyle and the Open Secret of His Life. By Henry Larkin. Demy 8vo, 14s.

CARPENTER, W. B., LL.D., M.D., F.R.S., etc.—The Principles of Mental Physiology. With their Applications to the Training and Discipline of the Mind, and the Study of its Morbid Conditions. Illustrated. Sixth Edition. 8vo, 12s.

Catholic Dictionary. Containing some Account of the Doctrine, Discipline, Rites, Ceremonies, Councils, and Religious Orders of the Catholic Church. By WILLIAM E. ADDIS and THOMAS ARNOLD, M.A. Third Edition. Demy 8vo, 21s.

CHEYNE, Rev. T. K.—The Prophecies of Isaiah. Translated with Critical Notes and Dissertations. 2 vols. Third Edition. Demy 8vo, 25s.

Circulating Capital. Being an Inquiry into the Fundamental Laws of Money. An Essay by an East India Merchant. Small crown 8vo, 6s.

CLAIRAUT.—Elements of Geometry. Translated by Dr. KAINES. With 145 Figures. Crown 8vo, 4s. 6d.

CLAPPERTON, Jane Hume.—Scientific Meliorism and the Evolution of Happiness. Large crown 8vo, 8s. 6d.

CLARKE, Rev. Henry James, A.K.C.—The Fundamental Science. Demy 8vo, 10s. 6d.

CLAYDEN, P. W.—Samuel Sharpe. Egyptologist and Translator of the Bible. Crown 8vo, 6s.

CLIFFORD, Samuel.—What Think Ye of the Christ? Crown 8vo, 6s.

CLODD, Edward, F.R.A.S.—The Childhood of the World: a Simple Account of Man in Early Times. Seventh Edition. Crown 8vo, 3s.
   A Special Edition for Schools. 1s.

   The Childhood of Religions. Including a Simple Account of the Birth and Growth of Myths and Legends. Eighth Thousand. Crown 8vo, 5s.
   A Special Edition for Schools. 1s. 6d.

   Jesus of Nazareth. With a brief sketch of Jewish History to the Time of His Birth. Small crown 8vo, 6s.

COGHLAN, J. Cole, D.D.—The Modern Pharisee and other Sermons. Edited by the Very Rev. H. H. DICKINSON, D.D., Dean of Chapel Royal, Dublin. New and Cheaper Edition. Crown 8vo, 7s. 6d.

COLE, George R. Fitz-Roy.—The Peruvians at Home. Crown 8vo, 6s.

COLERIDGE, Sara.—Memoir and Letters of Sara Coleridge. Edited by her Daughter. With Index. Cheap Edition. With Portrait. 7s. 6d.

Collects Exemplified. Being Illustrations from the Old and New Testaments of the Collects for the Sundays after Trinity. By the Author of "A Commentary on the Epistles and Gospels." Edited by the Rev. JOSEPH JACKSON. Crown 8vo, 5s.

CONNELL, A. K.—**Discontent and Danger in India.** Small crown 8vo, 3s. 6d.

The Economic Revolution of India. Crown 8vo, 4s. 6d.

COOK, Keningale, LL.D.—**The Fathers of Jesus.** A Study of the Lineage of the Christian Doctrine and Traditions. 2 vols. Demy 8vo, 28s.

CORY, William.—**A Guide to Modern English History.** Part I.—MDCCCXV.-MDCCCXXX. Demy 8vo, 9s. Part II.—MDCCCXXX.-MDCCCXXXV., 15s.

COTTERILL, H. B.—**An Introduction to the Study of Poetry.** Crown 8vo, 7s. 6d.

COTTON, H. J. S.—**New India, or India in Transition.** Third Edition. Crown 8vo, 4s. 6d.

COUTTS, Francis Burdett Money.—**The Training of the Instinct of Love.** With a Preface by the Rev. EDWARD THRING, M.A. Small crown 8vo, 2s. 6d.

COX, Rev. Sir George W., M.A., Bart.—**The Mythology of the Aryan Nations.** New Edition. Demy 8vo, 16s.

Tales of Ancient Greece. New Edition. Small crown 8vo, 6s.

A Manual of Mythology in the form of Question and Answer. New Edition. Fcap. 8vo, 3s.

An Introduction to the Science of Comparative Mythology and Folk-Lore. Second Edition. Crown 8vo, 7s. 6d.

COX, Rev. Sir G. W., M.A., Bart., and JONES, Eustace Hinton.—**Popular Romances of the Middle Ages.** Third Edition, in 1 vol. Crown 8vo, 6s.

COX, Rev. Samuel, D.D.—**A Commentary on the Book of Job.** With a Translation. Second Edition. Demy 8vo, 15s.

Salvator Mundi; or, Is Christ the Saviour of all Men? Tenth Edition. Crown 8vo, 5s.

The Larger Hope. A Sequel to "Salvator Mundi." Second Edition. 16mo, 1s.

The Genesis of Evil, and other Sermons, mainly expository. Third Edition. Crown 8vo, 6s.

Balaam. An Exposition and a Study. Crown 8vo, 5s.

Miracles. An Argument and a Challenge. Crown 8vo, 2s. 6d.

CRAVEN, Mrs.—**A Year's Meditations.** Crown 8vo, 6s.

CRAWFURD, *Oswald.*—**Portugal, Old and New.** With Illustrations and Maps. New and Cheaper Edition. Crown 8vo, 6s.

CROZIER, *John Beattie, M.B.*—**The Religion of the Future.** Crown 8vo, 6s.

CUNNINGHAM, *W., B.D.*—**Politics and Economics:** An Essay on the Nature of the Principles of Political Economy, together with a survey of Recent Legislation. Crown 8vo, 5s.

DANIELL, *Clarmont.*—**The Gold Treasure of India.** An Inquiry into its Amount, the Cause of its Accumulation, and the Proper Means of using it as Money. Crown 8vo, 5s.

Discarded Silver: a Plan for its Use as Money. Small crown, 8vo, 2s.

DANIEL, *Gerard.* **Mary Stuart: a Sketch and a Defence.** Crown 8vo, 5s.

DAVIDSON, *Rev. Samuel, D.D., LL.D.*—**Canon of the Bible:** Its Formation, History, and Fluctuations. Third and Revised Edition. Small crown 8vo, 5s.

The Doctrine of Last Things contained in the New Testament compared with the Notions of the Jews and the Statements of Church Creeds. Small crown 8vo, 3s. 6d.

DAWSON, *Geo., M.A.* **Prayers, with a Discourse on Prayer.** Edited by his Wife. First Series. Ninth Edition. Crown 8vo, 3s. 6d.

Prayers, with a Discourse on Prayer. Edited by GEORGE ST. CLAIR. Second Series. Crown 8vo, 6s.

Sermons on Disputed Points and Special Occasions. Edited by his Wife. Fourth Edition. Crown 8vo, 6s.

Sermons on Daily Life and Duty. Edited by his Wife. Fourth Edition. Crown 8vo, 6s.

The Authentic Gospel, and other Sermons. Edited by GEORGE ST. CLAIR, F.G.S. Third Edition. Crown 8vo, 6s.

Biographical Lectures. Edited by GEORGE ST. CLAIR, F.G.S. Large crown, 8vo, 7s. 6d.

DE JONCOURT, *Madame Marie.*—**Wholesome Cookery.** Third Edition. Crown 8vo, 3s. 6d.

Democracy in the Old World and the New. By the Author of "The Suez Canal, the Eastern Question, and Abyssinia," etc. Small crown 8vo, 2s. 6d.

DENT, *H. C.*—**A Year in Brazil.** With Notes on Religion, Meteorology, Natural History, etc. Maps and Illustrations. Demy 8vo, 18s.

Discourse on the Shedding of Blood, and The Laws of War. Demy 8vo, 2s. 6d.

DOUGLAS, Rev. Herman.—**Into the Deep ;** or, The Wonders of the Lord's Person. Crown 8vo, 2s. 6d.

DOWDEN, Edward, LL.D.—**Shakspere :** a Critical Study of his Mind and Art. Eighth Edition. Post 8vo, 12s.

> **Studies in Literature, 1789-1877.** Third Edition. Large post 8vo, 6s.

Dulce Domum. Fcap. 8vo, 5s.

DU MONCEL, Count.—**The Telephone, the Microphone, and the Phonograph.** With 74 Illustrations. Third Edition. Small crown 8vo, 5s.

DURUY, Victor.—**History of Rome and the Roman People.** Edited by Prof. MAHAFFY. With nearly 3000 Illustrations. 4to. 6 vols. in 12 parts, 30s. each vol.

EDGEWORTH, F. Y.—**Mathematical Psychics.** An Essay on the Application of Mathematics to Social Science. Demy 8vo, 7s. 6d.

Educational Code of the Prussian Nation, in its Present Form. In accordance with the Decisions of the Common Provincial Law, and with those of Recent Legislation. Crown 8vo, 2s. 6d.

Education Library. Edited by PHILIP MAGNUS :—

> **An Introduction to the History of Educational Theories.** By OSCAR BROWNING, M.A. Second Edition. 3s. 6d.

> **Old Greek Education.** By the Rev. Prof. MAHAFFY, M.A. Second Edition. 3s. 6d.

> **School Management.** Including a general view of the work of Education, Organization and Discipline. By JOSEPH LANDON. Fifth Edition. 6s.

EDWARDES, Major-General Sir Herbert B.—**Memorials of his Life and Letters.** By his Wife. With Portrait and Illustrations. 2 vols. Demy 8vo. 36s.

ELSDALE, Henry.—**Studies in Tennyson's Idylls.** Crown 8vo, 5s.

Emerson's (Ralph Waldo) Life. By OLIVER WENDELL HOLMES. English Copyright Edition. With Portrait. Crown 8vo, 6s.

Enoch the Prophet. The Book of. Archbishop LAURENCE's Translation, with an Introduction by the Author of "The Evolution of Christianity." Crown 8vo, 5s.

Eranus. A Collection of Exercises in the Alcaic and Sapphic Metres. Edited by F. W. CORNISH, Assistant Master at Eton. Second Edition. Crown 8vo, 2s.

EVANS, Mark.—**The Story of Our Father's Love,** told to Children. Sixth and Cheaper Edition. With Four Illustrations. Fcap. 8vo, 1s. 6d.

"Fan Kwae" at Canton before Treaty Days 1825-1844. By an old Resident. With Frontispiece. Crown 8vo, 5s.

Faith of the Unlearned, The. Authority, apart from the Sanction of Reason, an Insufficient Basis for It. By "One Unlearned." Crown 8vo, 6s.

FEIS, Jacob.—Shakspere and Montaigne. An Endeavour to Explain the Tendency of Hamlet from Allusions in Contemporary Works. Crown 8vo, 5s.

FLOREDICE, W. H.—A Month among the Mere Irish. Small crown 8vo. Second Edition. 3s. 6d.

Frank Leward. Edited by CHARLES BAMPTON. Crown 8vo, 7s. 6d.

FULLER. Rev. Morris.—The Lord's Day ; or, Christian Sunday. Its Unity, History, Philosophy, and Perpetual Obligation. Sermons. Demy 8vo, 10s. 6d.

GARDINER, Samuel R., and J. BASS MULLINGER, M.A.— Introduction to the Study of English History. Second Edition. Large crown 8vo, 9s.

GARDNER, Percy.—Quatre Bras, Ligny, and Waterloo. A Narrative of the Campaign in Belgium, 1815. With Maps and Plans. Demy 8vo, 16s.

GELDART, E. M.—Echoes of Truth. Sermons, with a Short Selection of Prayers and an Introductory Sketch, by the Rev. C. B. UPTON. Crown 8vo, 6s.

Genesis in Advance of Present Science. A Critical Investigation of Chapters I.-IX. By a Septuagenarian Beneficed Presbyter. Demy 8vo, 10s. 6d.

GEORGE, Henry.—Progress and Poverty : An Inquiry into the Causes of Industrial Depressions, and of Increase of Want with Increase of Wealth. The Remedy. Fifth Library Edition. Post 8vo, 7s. 6d. Cabinet Edition. Crown 8vo, 2s. 6d. Also a Cheap Edition. Limp cloth, 1s. 6d. Paper covers, 1s.

Protection, or Free Trade. An Examination of the Tariff Question, with especial regard to the Interests of Labour. Crown 8vo, 5s.

Social Problems. Fourth Thousand. Crown 8vo, 5s. Cheap Edition. Paper covers, 1s.

GLANVILL. Joseph.—Scepsis Scientifica : or, Confest Ignorance, the Way to Science : in an Essay of the Vanity of Dogmatizing and Confident Opinion. Edited, with Introductory Essay, by JOHN OWEN. Elzevir 8vo, printed on hand-made paper, 6s.

Glossary of Terms and Phrases. Edited by the Rev. H. PERCY SMITH and others. Second and Cheaper Edition. Medium 8vo, 7s. 6d.

GLOVER, F., M.A.—**Exempla Latina.** A First Construing Book, with Short Notes, Lexicon, and an Introduction to the Analysis of Sentences. Second Edition. Fcap. 8vo, 2s.

GOLDSMID, Sir Francis Henry, Bart., Q.C., M.P.—**Memoir of.** With Portrait. Second Edition, Revised. Crown 8vo, 6s.

GOODENOUGH, Commodore J. G.—**Memoir of,** with Extracts from his Letters and Journals. Edited by his Widow. With Steel Engraved Portrait. Third Edition. Crown 8vo, 5s.

GORDON, Major-Genl. C. G.—**His Journals at Kartoum.** Printed from the original MS. With Introduction and Notes by A. Egmont Hake. Portrait, 2 Maps, and 30 Illustrations. Two vols., demy 8vo, 21s. Also a Cheap Edition in 1 vol., 6s.

Gordon's (General) Last Journal. A Facsimile of the last Journal received in England from General Gordon. Reproduced by Photo-lithography. Imperial 4to, £3 3s.

Events in his Life. From the Day of his Birth to the Day of his Death. By Sir H. W. Gordon. With Maps and Illustrations. Demy 8vo, 18s.

GOSSE, Edmund.—**Seventeenth Century Studies.** A Contribution to the History of English Poetry. Demy 8vo, 10s. 6d.

GOULD, Rev. S. Baring, M.A.—**Germany, Present and Past.** New and Cheaper Edition. Large crown 8vo, 7s. 6d.

GOWAN, Major Walter E.—**A. Ivanoff's Russian Grammar.** (16th Edition.) Translated, enlarged, and arranged for use of Students of the Russian Language. Demy 8vo, 6s.

GOWER, Lord Ronald. **My Reminiscences.** Miniature Edition, printed on hand-made paper, limp parchment antique, 10s. 6d.

Last Days of Mary Antoinette. An Historical Sketch. With Portrait and Facsimiles. Fcap. 4to, 10s. 6d.

Notes of a Tour from Brindisi to Yokohama, 1883–1884. Fcap. 8vo, 2s. 6d.

GRAHAM, William, M.A.—**The Creed of Science,** Religious, Moral, and Social. Second Edition, Revised. Crown 8vo, 6s.

The Social Problem, in its Economic, Moral, **and Political Aspects.** Demy 8vo, 14s.

GRAY, Rowland.—**In Sunny Switzerland.** A Tale of Six Weeks. Second Edition. Small crown 8vo, 5s.

Lindenblumen and other Stories. Small crown 8vo, 5s.

GRIMLEY, Rev. H. N., M.A.—**Tremadoc Sermons, chiefly on the Spiritual Body, the Unseen World, and the Divine Humanity.** Fourth Edition. Crown 8vo, 6s.

GUSTAFSON, Alex.—**The Foundation of Death.** Third Edition. Crown 8vo, 5s.

GUSTAFSON, *Alex.—continued.*

> Some Thoughts on Moderation. Reprinted from a Paper read at the Reeve Mission Room, Manchester Square, June 8, 1885. Crown 8vo, 1s.

HADDON, *Caroline.*—The Larger Life, Studies in Hinton's Ethics. Crown 8vo, 5s.

HAECKEL, *Prof. Ernst.*—The History of Creation. Translation revised by Professor E. RAY LANKESTER, M.A., F.R.S. With Coloured Plates and Genealogical Trees of the various groups of both Plants and Animals. 2 vols. Third Edition. Post 8vo, 32s.

> The History of the Evolution of Man. With numerous Illustrations. 2 vols. Post 8vo, 32s.

> A Visit to Ceylon. Post 8vo, 7s. 6d.

> Freedom in Science and Teaching. With a Prefatory Note by T. H. HUXLEY, F.R.S. Crown 8vo, 5s.

HALF-CROWN SERIES :—

> A Lost Love. By ANNA C. OGLE [Ashford Owen].

> Sister Dora : a Biography. By MARGARET LONSDALE.

> True Words for Brave Men : a Book for Soldiers and Sailors. By the late CHARLES KINGSLEY.

> Notes of Travel : being Extracts from the Journals of Count VON MOLTKE.

> English Sonnets. Collected and Arranged by J. DENNIS.

> Home Songs for Quiet Hours. By the Rev. Canon R. H. BAYNES.

Hamilton, Memoirs of Arthur, B.A., of Trinity College, Cambridge. Crown 8vo, 6s.

HARRIS, *William.*—The History of the Radical Party in Parliament. Demy 8vo, 15s.

HARROP, *Robert.*—Bolingbroke. A Political Study and Criticism. Demy 8vo, 14s.

HART, *Rev. J. W. T.*—The Autobiography of Judas Iscariot. A Character Study. Crown 8vo, 3s. 6d.

HAWEIS, *Rev. H. R., M.A.*—Current Coin. Materialism—The Devil—Crime—Drunkenness—Pauperism—Emotion—Recreation —The Sabbath. Fifth Edition. Crown 8vo, 5s.

> Arrows in the Air. Fifth Edition. Crown 8vo, 5s.

> Speech in Season. Fifth Edition. Crown 8vo, 5s.

> Thoughts for the Times. Thirteenth Edition. Crown 8vo, 5s.

> Unsectarian Family Prayers. New Edition. Fcap. 8vo, 1s. 6d.

HAWKINS, Edwards Comerford.—**Spirit and Form.** Sermons preached in the Parish Church of Leatherhead. Crown 8vo, 6s.

HAWTHORNE, Nathaniel.—**Works.** Complete in Twelve Volumes. Large post 8vo, 7s. 6d. each volume.

VOL. I. TWICE-TOLD TALES.
II. MOSSES FROM AN OLD MANSE.
III. THE HOUSE OF THE SEVEN GABLES, AND THE SNOW IMAGE.
IV. THE WONDERBOOK, TANGLEWOOD TALES, AND GRANDFATHER'S CHAIR.
V. THE SCARLET LETTER, AND THE BLITHEDALE ROMANCE.
VI. THE MARBLE FAUN. [Transformation.]
VII. ⎱ OUR OLD HOME, AND ENGLISH NOTE-BOOKS.
VIII. ⎰
IX. AMERICAN NOTE-BOOKS.
X. FRENCH AND ITALIAN NOTE-BOOKS.
XI. SEPTIMIUS FELTON, THE DOLLIVER ROMANCE, FANSHAWE, AND, IN AN APPENDIX, THE ANCESTRAL FOOTSTEP.
XII. TALES AND ESSAYS, AND OTHER PAPERS, WITH A BIOGRAPHICAL SKETCH OF HAWTHORNE.

HEATH, Francis George.—**Autumnal Leaves.** Third and cheaper Edition. Large crown 8vo, 6s.

Sylvan Winter. With 70 Illustrations. Large crown 8vo, 14s.

HENNESSY, Sir John Pope.—**Ralegh in Ireland.** With his Letters on Irish Affairs and some Contemporary Documents. Large crown 8vo, printed on hand-made paper, parchment, 10s. 6d.

HENRY, Philip.—**Diaries and Letters of.** Edited by MATTHEW HENRY LEE, M.A. Large crown 8vo, 7s. 6d.

HINTON, J.—**Life and Letters.** With an Introduction by Sir W. W. GULL, Bart., and Portrait engraved on Steel by C. H. Jeens. Fifth Edition. Crown 8vo, 8s. 6d.

Philosophy and Religion. Selections from the Manuscripts of the late James Hinton. Edited by CAROLINE HADDON. Second Edition. Crown 8vo, 5s.

The Law Breaker, and The Coming of the Law. Edited by MARGARET HINTON. Crown 8vo, 6s.

The Mystery of Pain. New Edition. Fcap. 8vo, 1s.

Hodson of Hodson's Horse; or, Twelve Years of a Soldier's Life in India. Being extracts from the Letters of the late Major W. S. R. Hodson. With a Vindication from the Attack of Mr. Bosworth Smith. Edited by his brother, G. H. HODSON, M.A. Fourth Edition. Large crown 8vo, 5s.

HOLTHAM, E. G.—**Eight Years in Japan, 1873-1881.** Work, Travel, and Recreation. With three Maps. Large crown 8vo, 9s.

Homology of Economic Justice. An Essay by an East India Merchant. Small crown 8vo, 5s.

HOOPER, Mary.—**Little Dinners: How to Serve them with Elegance and Economy.** Twentieth Edition. Crown 8vo, 2s. 6d.

Cookery for Invalids, Persons of Delicate Digestion, and Children. Fifth Edition. Crown 8vo, 2s. 6d.

Every-Day Meals. Being Economical and Wholesome Recipes for Breakfast, Luncheon, and Supper. Sixth Edition. Crown 8vo, 2s. 6d.

HOPKINS, Ellice.—**Work amongst Working Men.** Sixth Edition. Crown 8vo, 3s. 6d.

HORNADAY, W. T.—**Two Years in a Jungle.** With Illustrations. Demy 8vo, 21s.

HOSPITALIER, E.—**The Modern Applications of Electricity.** Translated and Enlarged by JULIUS MAIER, Ph.D. 2 vols. Second Edition, Revised, with many additions and numerous Illustrations. Demy 8vo, 12s. 6d. each volume.

    VOL. I.—Electric Generators, Electric Light.
    VOL. II.—Telephone : Various Applications : Electrical Transmission of Energy.

HOWARD, Robert, M.A.—**The Church of England and other Religious Communions.** A course of Lectures delivered in the Parish Church of Clapham. Crown 8vo, 7s. 6d.

HUMPHREY, Rev. William.—**The Bible and Belief.** A Letter to a Friend. Small Crown 8vo, 2s. 6d.

HUNTER, William C.—**Bits of Old China.** Small crown 8vo, 6s.

HUNTINGFORD, Rev. E., D.C.L.—**The Apocalypse.** With a Commentary and Introductory Essay. Demy 8vo, 5s.

HUTCHINSON, H.—**Thought Symbolism, and Grammatic Illusions.** Being a Treatise on the Nature, Purpose, and Material of Speech. Crown 8vo, 2s. 6d.

HUTTON, Rev. C. F.—**Unconscious Testimony ; or, The Silent Witness of the Hebrew to the Truth of the Historical Scriptures.** Crown 8vo, 2s. 6d.

HYNDMAN, H. M.—**The Historical Basis of Socialism in England.** Large crown 8vo, 8s. 6d.

IDDESLEIGH, Earl of.—**The Pleasures, Dangers, and Uses of Desultory Reading.** Fcap. 8vo, in Whatman paper cover, 1s.

IM THURN, Everard F.—**Among the Indians** of Guiana. Being Sketches, chiefly anthropologic, from the Interior of British Guiana. With 53 Illustrations and a Map. Demy 8vo, 18s.

JACCOUD, Prof. S.—The Curability and Treatment of Pulmonary Phthisis. Translated and edited by MONTAGU LUBBOCK, M.D. Demy 8vo, 15s.

Jaunt in a Junk: A Ten Days' Cruise in Indian Seas. Large crown 8vo, 7s. 6d.

JENKINS, E., and RAYMOND, J.—The Architect's Legal Handbook. Third Edition, revised. Crown 8vo, 6s.

JENKINS, Rev. Canon R. C.—Heraldry : English and Foreign. With a Dictionary of Heraldic Terms and 156 Illustrations. Small crown 8vo, 3s. 6d.

JERVIS, Rev. W. Henley.—The Gallican Church and the Revolution. A Sequel to the History of the Church of France, from the Concordat of Bologna to the Revolution. Demy 8vo, 18s.

JOEL, L.—A Consul's Manual and Shipowner's and Shipmaster's Practical Guide in their Transactions Abroad. With Definitions of Nautical, Mercantile, and Legal Terms ; a Glossary of Mercantile Terms in English, French, German, Italian, and Spanish ; Tables of the Money, Weights, and Measures of the Principal Commercial Nations and their Equivalents in British Standards ; and Forms of Consular and Notarial Acts. Demy 8vo, 12s.

JOHNSTON, H. H., F.Z.S.—The Kilima-njaro Expedition. A Record of Scientific Exploration in Eastern Equatorial Africa, and a General Description of the Natural History, Languages, and Commerce of the Kilima-njaro District. With 6 Maps, and over 80 Illustrations by the Author. Demy 8vo, 21s.

JOYCE, P. W., LL.D., etc.—Old Celtic Romances. Translated from the Gaelic. Crown 8vo, 7s. 6d.

KAUFMANN, Rev. M., B.A.—Socialism : its Nature, its Dangers, and its Remedies considered. Crown 8vo, 7s. 6d.

Utopias ; or, Schemes of Social Improvement, from Sir Thomas More to Karl Marx. Crown 8vo, 5s.

KAY, David, F.R.G.S.—Education and Educators. Crown 8vo, 7s. 6d.

KAY, Joseph.—Free Trade in Land. Edited by his Widow. With Preface by the Right Hon. JOHN BRIGHT, M.P. Seventh Edition. Crown 8vo, 5s.

⁂ Also a cheaper edition, without the Appendix, but with a Revise of Recent Changes in the Land Laws of England, by the RIGHT HON. G. OSBORNE MORGAN, Q.C., M.P. Cloth, 1s. 6d. Paper covers, 1s.

KELKE, W. H. H.—An Epitome of English Grammar for the Use of Students. Adapted to the London Matriculation Course and Similar Examinations. Crown 8vo, 4s. 6d.

KEMPIS, Thomas à.—**Of the Imitation of Christ.** Parchment Library Edition.—Parchment or cloth, 6s. ; vellum, 7s. 6d. The Red Line Edition, fcap. 8vo, red edges, 2s. 6d. The Cabinet Edition, small 8vo, cloth limp, 1s. ; cloth boards, red edges, 1s. 6d. The Miniature Edition, red edges, 32mo, 1s.

*** All the above Editions may be had in various extra bindings.

KETTLEWELL, Rev. S.—**Thomas à Kempis and the Brothers** of Common **Life.** With Portrait. Crown 8vo, 7s. 6d.

KIDD, Joseph, M.D.—**The Laws of Therapeutics ;** or, the Science and Art of Medicine. Second Edition. Crown 8vo, 6s.

KINGSFORD, Anna, M.D.—**The Perfect Way in Diet.** A Treatise advocating a Return to the Natural and Ancient Food of our Race. Second Edition. Small crown 8vo, 2s.

KINGSLEY, Charles, M.A.—**Letters and Memories of his Life.** Edited by his Wife. With two Steel Engraved Portraits, and Vignettes on Wood. Fifteenth Cabinet Edition. 2 vols. Crown 8vo, 12s.

*** Also a People's Edition, in one volume. With Portrait. Crown 8vo, 6s.

All Saints' Day, and other Sermons. Edited by the Rev. W. HARRISON. Third Edition. Crown 8vo, 7s. 6d.

True Words for Brave Men. A Book for Soldiers' and Sailors' Libraries. Eleventh Edition. Crown 8vo, 2s. 6d.

KNOX, Alexander A.—**The New Playground ;** or, Wanderings in Algeria. New and Cheaper Edition. Large crown 8vo, 6s.

Land Concentration and Irresponsibility of Political Power, as causing the Anomaly of a Widespread State of Want by the Side of the Vast Supplies of Nature. Crown 8vo, 5s.

LANDON, Joseph.—**School Management :** Including a General View of the Work of Education, Organization, and Discipline. Fifth Edition. Crown 8vo, 6s.

LEE, Rev. F. G., D.C.L.—**The Other World ;** or, Glimpses of the Supernatural. 2 vols. A New Edition. Crown 8vo, 15s.

Letters from an Unknown Friend. By the Author of "Charles Lowder." With a Preface by the Rev. W. H. CLEAVER. Fcap. 8vo, 1s.

Leward, Frank. Edited by CHARLES BAMPTON. Crown 8vo, 7s. 6d.

LEWIS, Edward Dillon.—**A Draft Code of Criminal Law and Procedure.** Demy 8vo, 21s.

Life of a Prig. By ONE. Third Edition. Fcap. 8vo, 3s. 6d.

LILLIE, Arthur, M.R.A.S.—**The Popular Life of Buddha.** Containing an Answer to the Hibbert Lectures of 1881. With Illustrations. Crown 8vo, 6s.

LLOYD, Walter.—**The Hope of the World** : An Essay on Universal Redemption. Crown Svo, 5*s.*

LONGFELLOW, H. Wadsworth.—**Life.** By his Brother, SAMUEL LONGFELLOW. With Portraits and Illustrations. 2 vols. Demy Svo, 28*s.*

LONSDALE, Margaret.—**Sister Dora** : a Biography. With Portrait. Cheap Edition. Small crown Svo, 2*s.* 6*d.*

    George Eliot: Thoughts upon her Life, her Books, and Herself. Second Edition. Small crown Svo, 1*s.* 6*d.*

LOUNSBURY, Thomas R.—**James Fenimore Cooper.** With Portrait. Crown Svo, 5*s.*

LOWDER, Charles.—**A Biography.** By the Author of "St. Teresa." New and Cheaper Edition. Crown Svo. With Portrait. 3*s.* 6*d.*

LÜCKES, Eva C. E.—**Lectures on General Nursing,** delivered to the Probationers of the London Hospital Training School for Nurses. Crown Svo, 2*s.* 6*d.*

LYALL, William Rowe, D.D.—**Propædeia Prophetica ;** or, The Use and Design of the Old Testament Examined. New Edition. With Notices by GEORGE C. PEARSON, M.A., Hon. Canon of Canterbury. Demy Svo, 10*s.* 6*d.*

LYTTON, Edward Bulwer, Lord.—**Life, Letters and Literary Remains.** By his Son, the EARL OF LYTTON. With Portraits, Illustrations and Facsimiles. Demy Svo. Vols. I. and II., 32*s.*

MACAULAY, G. C.—**Francis Beaumont** : A Critical Study. Crown Svo, 5*s.*

MAC CALLUM, M. W.—**Studies in Low German and High German Literature.** Crown Svo, 6*s.*

MACHIAVELLI, Niccolò.—**Life and Times.** By Prof. VILLARI. Translated by LINDA VILLARI. 4 vols. Large post Svo, 48*s.*

MACHIAVELLI, Niccolò.—**Discourses on the First Decade of Titus Livius.** Translated from the Italian by NINIAN HILL THOMSON, M.A. Large crown Svo, 12*s.*

    The Prince. Translated from the Italian by N. H. T. Small crown Svo, printed on hand-made paper, bevelled boards, 6*s.*

MACKENZIE, Alexander.—**How India is Governed.** Being an Account of England's Work in India. Small crown Svo, 2*s.*

MAGNUS, Mrs.—**About the Jews since Bible Times.** From the Babylonian Exile till the English Exodus. Small crown 8vo, 6*s.*

MAGUIRE, Thomas.—**Lectures on Philosophy.** Demy Svo, 9*s.*

MAIR, R. S., M.D., F.R.C.S.E.—**The Medical Guide for Anglo-Indians.** Being a Compendium of Advice to Europeans in India, relating to the Preservation and Regulation of Health. With a Supplement on the Management of Children in India. Second Edition. Crown Svo, limp cloth, 3*s.* 6*d.*

C

MALDEN, Henry Elliot.—Vienna, **1683**. The History and Consequences of the Defeat of the Turks before Vienna, September 12th, 1683, by John Sobieski, King of Poland, and Charles Leopold, Duke of Lorraine. Crown 8vo, 4s. 6d.

Many Voices. A volume of Extracts from the Religious Writers of Christendom from the First to the Sixteenth Century. With Biographical Sketches. Crown 8vo, cloth extra, red edges, 6s.

MARKHAM, Capt. Albert Hastings, R.N.—The Great Frozen Sea : A Personal Narrative of the Voyage of the *Alert* during the Arctic Expedition of 1875-6. With 6 Full-page Illustrations, 2 Maps, and 27 Woodcuts. Sixth and Cheaper Edition. Crown 8vo, 6s.

MARTINEAU, Gertrude.—Outline Lessons on Morals. Small crown 8vo, 3s. 6d.

MAUDSLEY, H., M.D.—Body and Will. Being an Essay concerning Will, in its Metaphysical, Physiological, and Pathological Aspects. 8vo, 12s.

    Natural **Causes** and **Su**pernatural Seemings. **Crown** 8vo, 6s.

McGRATH, Terence.—Pictures from Ireland. **New** and Cheaper Edition. Crown 8vo, **2s.**

MEREDITH, M.A.—Theotokos, the **Example for** Woman. Dedicated, by permission, to Lady Agnes Wood. Revised by the Venerable Archdeacon DENISON. 32mo, limp cloth, 1s. 6d.

MILLER, Edward.—The His**tory** and **Doctrines of** Irvingism ; or, The so-called Catholic and Apostolic Church. 2 vols. Large post 8vo, 25s.

    The **Church in Relation to the State.** Large crown 8vo, 7s. 6d.

MITCHELL, Lucy M.—**A** History **of** Ancient Sculpture. **With** numerous Illustrations, including 6 Plates in Phototype. **Super** royal 8vo, 42s.

MITFORD, Bertram.—**T**hrough the **Zulu** Country. Its **Battle**-fields and its People. With Five Illustrations. Demy 8vo, 14s.

MOCKLER, E.—A Grammar of the **Baloochee** Language, as it is spoken in Makran (Ancient Gedrosia), in the Persia-Arabic and Roman characters. Fcap. 8vo, 5s.

MOLESWORTH, Rev. W. Nassau, M.A.—History **of the Church of** England from 1660. Large crown 8vo, 7s. 6d.

MORELL, J. R.—Euclid Simplified in Method **and Language.** Being a Manual of Geometry. Compiled from the most important French Works, approved by the University of Paris and the Minister of Public Instruction. Fcap. 8vo, 2s. 6d.

MORGAN, C. Lloyd.—**The Springs of Conduct.** An Essay in Evolution. **Large crown 8vo, cloth, 7s. 6d.**

MORRIS, *George.*—The Duality of all Divine Truth in our Lord Jesus Christ. For God's Self-manifestation in the Impartation of the Divine Nature to Man. Large crown 8vo, 7s. 6d.

MORSE, E. S., Ph.D.—First Book of Zoology. With numerous Illustrations. New and Cheaper Edition. Crown 8vo, 2s. 6d.

NELSON, J. H., M.A.—A Prospectus of the Scientific Study of the Hindû Law. Demy 8vo, 9s.

NEWMAN, *Cardinal.*—Characteristics from the Writings of. Being Selections from his various Works. Arranged with the Author's personal Approval. Seventh Edition. With Portrait. Crown 8vo, 6s.

₊ A Portrait of Cardinal Newman, mounted for framing, can be had, 2s. 6d.

NEWMAN, *Francis William.*—Essays on Diet. Small crown 8vo, cloth limp, 2s.

New Truth and the Old Faith: Are they Incompatible? By a Scientific Layman. Demy 8vo, 10s. 6d.

New Social Teachings. By POLITICUS. Small crown 8vo, 5s.

NICOLS, *Arthur, F.G.S., F.R.G.S.*—Chapters from the Physical History of the Earth: an Introduction to Geology and Palæontology. With numerous Illustrations. Crown 8vo, 5s.

NOEL, *The Hon. Roden.*—Essays on Poetry and Poets. Demy 8vo, 12s.

NOPS, *Marianne.*—Class Lessons on Euclid. Part I. containing the First Two Books of the Elements. Crown 8vo, 2s. 6d.

Nuces: EXERCISES ON THE SYNTAX OF THE PUBLIC SCHOOL LATIN PRIMER. New Edition in Three Parts. Crown 8vo, each 1s.

₊ The Three Parts can also be had bound together, 3s.

OATES, *Frank, F.R.G.S.*—Matabele Land and the Victoria Falls. A Naturalist's Wanderings in the Interior of South Africa. Edited by C. G. OATES, B.A. With numerous Illustrations and 4 Maps. Demy 8vo, 21s.

O'CONNOR, T. P., M.P.—The Parnell Movement. With a Sketch of Irish Parties from 1843. Large crown 8vo, 7s. 6d.

OGLE, W., M.D., F.R.C.P.—Aristotle on the Parts of Animals. Translated, with Introduction and Notes. Royal 8vo, 12s. 6d.

O'HAGAN, *Lord, K.P.*—Occasional Papers and Addresses. Large crown 8vo, 7s. 6d.

O'MEARA, *Kathleen.*—Frederic Ozanam, Professor of the Sorbonne: His Life and Work. Second Edition. Crown 8vo, 7s. 6d.

Henri Perreyve and his Counsels to the Sick. Small crown 8vo, 5s.

One and a Half in Norway. A Chronicle of Small Beer. By Either and Both. Small crown 8vo, 3s. 6d.

O'NEIL, *the late Rev.* Lord.—Sermons. With Memoir and Portrait. Crown 8vo, 6s.

Essays and Addresses. Crown 8vo, 5s.

Only Passport to Heaven, The. By One who has it. Small crown 8vo, 1s. 6d.

OSBORNE, *Rev. W. A.*—The Revised Version of the New Testament. A Critical Commentary, with Notes upon the Text. Crown 8vo, 5s.

OTTLEY, *H. Bickersteth.*—The Great Dilemma. Christ His Own Witness or His Own Accuser. Six Lectures. Second Edition. Crown 8vo, 3s. 6d.

Our Public Schools—Eton, Harrow, Winchester, Rugby, Westminster, Marlborough, The Charterhouse. Crown 8vo, 6s.

OWEN, *F. M.*—John Keats: a Study. Crown 8vo, 6s.

Across the Hills. Small crown 8vo, 1s. 6d.

OWEN, *Rev. Robert, B.D.*—Sanctorale Catholicum; or, Book of Saints. With Notes, Critical, Exegetical, and Historical. Demy 8vo, 18s.

OXONIENSIS.—Romanism, Protestantism, Anglicanism. Being a Layman's View of some questions of the Day. Together with Remarks on Dr. Littledale's "Plain Reasons against joining the Church of Rome." Crown 8vo, 3s. 6d.

PALMER, *the late William.*—Notes of a Visit to Russia in 1840-1841. Selected and arranged by JOHN H. CARDINAL NEWMAN, with Portrait. Crown 8vo, 8s. 6d.

Early Christian Symbolism. A Series of Compositions from Fresco Paintings, Glasses, and Sculptured Sarcophagi. Edited by the Rev. Provost NORTHCOTE, D.D., and the Rev. Canon BROWNLOW, M.A. With Coloured Plates, folio, 42s., or with Plain Plates, folio, 25s.

Parchment Library. Choicely Printed on hand-made paper, limp parchment antique or cloth, 6s.; vellum, 7s. 6d. each volume.

The Poetical Works of John Milton. 2 vols.

Letters and Journals of Jonathan Swift. Selected and edited, with a Commentary and Notes, by STANLEY LANE POOLE.

De Quincey's Confessions of an English Opium Eater. Reprinted from the First Edition. Edited by RICHARD GARNETT.

The Gospel according to Matthew, Mark, and Luke.

Parchment Library—*continued.*

Selections from the Prose Writings of Jonathan Swift. With a Preface and Notes by STANLEY LANE-POOLE and Portrait.

English Sacred Lyrics.

Sir Joshua Reynolds's Discourses. Edited by EDMUND GOSSE.

Selections from Milton's Prose Writings. Edited by ERNEST MYERS.

The Book of Psalms. Translated by the Rev. T. K. CHEYNE, M.A.

The Vicar of Wakefield. With Preface and Notes by AUSTIN DOBSON.

English Comic Dramatists. Edited by OSWALD CRAWFURD.

English Lyrics.

The Sonnets of John Milton. Edited by MARK PATTISON. With Portrait after Vertue.

French Lyrics. Selected and Annotated by GEORGE SAINTSBURY. With a Miniature Frontispiece designed and etched by H. G. Glindoni.

Fables by Mr. John Gay. With Memoir by AUSTIN DOBSON, and an Etched Portrait from an unfinished Oil Sketch by Sir Godfrey Kneller.

Select Letters of Percy Bysshe Shelley. Edited, with an Introduction, by RICHARD GARNETT.

The Christian Year. Thoughts in Verse for the Sundays and Holy Days throughout the Year. With Miniature Portrait of the Rev. J. Keble, after a Drawing by G. Richmond, R.A.

Shakspere's Works. Complete in Twelve Volumes.

Eighteenth Century Essays. Selected and Edited by AUSTIN DOBSON. With a Miniature Frontispiece by R. Caldecott.

Q. Horati Flacci Opera. Edited by F. A. CORNISH, Assistant Master at Eton. With a Frontispiece after a design by L. Alma Tadema, etched by Leopold Lowenstam.

Edgar Allan Poe's Poems. With an Essay on his Poetry by ANDREW LANG, and a Frontispiece by Linley Sambourne.

Shakspere's Sonnets. Edited by EDWARD DOWDEN. With a Frontispiece etched by Leopold Lowenstam, after the Death Mask.

English Odes. Selected by EDMUND GOSSE. With Frontispiece on India paper by Hamo Thornycroft, A.R.A.

Parchment Library—*continued.*

Of the Imitation of Christ. By THOMAS À KEMPIS. A revised Translation. With Frontispiece on India paper, from a Design by W. B. Richmond.

Poems : Selected from PERCY BYSSHE SHELLEY. Dedicated to Lady Shelley. With a Preface by RICHARD GARNETT and a Miniature Frontispiece.

PARSLOE, Joseph.—Our Railways. Sketches, Historical and Descriptive. With Practical Information as to Fares and Rates, etc., and a Chapter on Railway Reform. Crown 8vo, 6s.

PASCAL, Blaise.—The Thoughts of. Translated from the Text of Auguste Molinier, by C. KEGAN PAUL. Large crown 8vo, with Frontispiece, printed on hand-made paper, parchment antique, or cloth, 12s. ; vellum, 15s.

PAUL, Alexander.—Short Parliaments. A History of the National Demand for frequent General Elections. Small crown 8vo, 3s. 6d.

PAUL, C. Kegan.—Biographical Sketches. Printed on hand-made paper, bound in buckram. Second Edition. Crown 8vo, 7s. 6d.

PEARSON, Rev. S.—Week-day Living. A Book for Young Men and Women. Second Edition. Crown 8vo, 5s.

PENRICE, Major J.—Arabic and English Dictionary of the Koran. 4to, 21s.

PESCHEL, Dr. Oscar.—The Races of Man and their Geographical Distribution. Second Edition. Large crown 8vo, 9s.

PHIPSON, E.—The Animal Lore of Shakspeare's Time. Including Quadrupeds, Birds, Reptiles, Fish and Insects. Large post 8vo, 9s.

PIDGEON, D.—An Engineer's Holiday ; or, Notes of a Round Trip from Long. 0° to 0°. New and Cheaper Edition. Large crown 8vo, 7s. 6d.

Old World Questions and New World Answers. Second Edition. Large crown 8vo, 7s. 6d.

Plain Thoughts for Men. Eight Lectures delivered at Forester's Hall, Clerkenwell, during the London Mission, 1884. Crown 8vo, cloth, 1s. 6d ; paper covers, 1s.

POE, Edgar Allan.—Works of. With an Introduction and a Memoir by RICHARD HENRY STODDARD. In 6 vols. With Frontispieces and Vignettes. Large crown 8vo, 6s. each.

POPE, J. Buckingham. — Railway Rates and Radical Rule. Trade Questions as Election Tests. Crown 8vo, 2s. 6d.

PRICE, Prof. Bonamy. — Chapters on Practical Political Economy. Being the Substance of Lectures delivered before the University of Oxford. New and Cheaper Edition. Crown 8vo, 5s.

Pulpit Commentary, The. (Old Testament Series.) Edited by the Rev. J. S. EXELL, M.A., and the Rev. Canon H. D. M. SPENCE.

Genesis. By the Rev. T. WHITELAW, M.A. With Homilies by the Very Rev. J. F. MONTGOMERY, D.D., Rev. Prof. R. A. REDFORD, M.A., LL.B., Rev. F. HASTINGS, Rev. W. ROBERTS, M.A. An Introduction to the Study of the Old Testament by the Venerable Archdeacon FARRAR, D.D., F.R.S.; and Introductions to the Pentateuch by the Right Rev. H. COTTERILL, D.D., and Rev. T. WHITELAW, M.A. Eighth Edition. 1 vol., 15*s.*

Exodus. By the Rev. Canon RAWLINSON. With Homilies by Rev. J. ORR, Rev. D. YOUNG, B.A., Rev. C. A. GOODHART, Rev. J. URQUHART, and the Rev. H. T. ROBJOHNS. Fourth Edition. 2 vols., 18*s.*

Leviticus. By the Rev. Prebendary MEYRICK, M.A. With Introductions by the Rev. R. COLLINS, Rev. Professor A. CAVE, and Homilies by Rev. Prof. REDFORD, LL.B., Rev. J. A. MACDONALD, Rev. W. CLARKSON, B.A., Rev. S. R. ALDRIDGE, LL.B., and Rev. McCHEYNE EDGAR. Fourth Edition. 15*s.*

Numbers. By the Rev. R. WINTERBOTHAM, LL.B. With Homilies by the Rev. Professor W. BINNIE, D.D., Rev. E. S. PROUT, M.A., Rev. D. YOUNG, Rev. J. WAITE, and an Introduction by the Rev. THOMAS WHITELAW, M.A. Fourth Edition. 15*s.*

Deuteronomy. By the Rev. W. L. ALEXANDER, D.D. With Homilies by Rev. C. CLEMANCE, D.D., Rev. J. ORR, B.D., Rev. R. M. EDGAR, M.A., Rev. D. DAVIES, M.A. Fourth edition. 15*s.*

Joshua. By Rev. J. J. LIAS, M.A. With Homilies by Rev. S. R. ALDRIDGE, LL.B., Rev. R. GLOVER, REV. E. DE PRESSENSÉ, D.D., Rev. J. WAITE, B.A., Rev. W. F. ADENEY, M.A.; and an Introduction by the Rev. A. PLUMMER, M.A. Fifth Edition. 12*s.* 6*d.*

Judges and Ruth. By the Bishop of Bath and Wells, and Rev. J. MORISON, D.D. With Homilies by Rev. A. F. MUIR, M.A., Rev. W. F. ADENEY, M.A., Rev. W. M. STATHAM, and Rev. Professor J. THOMSON, M.A. Fifth Edition. 10*s.* 6*d.*

1 Samuel. By the Very Rev. R. P. SMITH, D.D. With Homilies by Rev. DONALD FRASER, D.D., Rev. Prof. CHAPMAN, and Rev. B. DALE. Sixth Edition. 15*s.*

1 Kings. By the Rev. JOSEPH HAMMOND, LL.B. With Homilies by the Rev. E. DE PRESSENSÉ, D.D., Rev. J. WAITE, B.A., Rev. A. ROWLAND, LL.B., Rev. J. A. MACDONALD, and Rev. J. URQUHART. Fourth Edition. 15*s.*

Pulpit Commentary, The—*continued.*

1 Chronicles. By the Rev. Prof. P. C. BARKER, M.A., LL.B. With Homilies by Rev. Prof. J. R. THOMSON, M.A., Rev. R. TUCK, B.A., Rev. W. CLARKSON, B.A., Rev. F. WHITFIELD, M.A., and Rev. RICHARD GLOVER. 15s.

Ezra, Nehemiah, and Esther. By Rev. Canon G. RAWLINSON, M.A. With Homilies by Rev. Prof. J. R. THOMSON, M.A., Rev. Prof. R. A. REDFORD, LL.B., M.A., Rev. W. S. LEWIS, M.A., Rev. J. A. MACDONALD, Rev. A. MACKENNAL, B.A., Rev. W. CLARKSON, B.A., Rev. F. HASTINGS, Rev. W. DINWIDDIE, LL.B., Rev. Prof. ROWLANDS, B.A., Rev. G. WOOD, B.A., Rev. Prof. P. C. BARKER, M.A., LL.B., and the Rev. J. S. EXELL, M.A. Sixth Edition. 1 vol., 12s. 6d.

Jeremiah. (Vol. I.) By the Rev. T. K. CHEYNE, M.A. With Homilies by the Rev. W. F. ADENEY, M.A., Rev. A. F. MUIR, M.A., Rev. S. CONWAY, B.A., Rev. J. WAITE, B.A., and Rev. D. YOUNG, B.A. Second Edition. 15s.

Jeremiah (Vol. II.) and Lamentations. By Rev. T. K. CHEYNE, M.A. With Homilies by Rev. Prof. J. R. THOMSON, M.A., Rev. W. F. ADENEY, M.A., Rev. A. F. MUIR, M.A., Rev. S. CONWAY, B.A., Rev. D. YOUNG, B.A. 15s.

Pulpit Commentary, The. (New Testament Series.)

St. Mark. By Very Rev. E. BICKERSTETH, D.D., Dean of Lichfield. With Homilies by Rev. Prof. THOMSON, M.A., Rev. Prof. GIVEN, M.A., Rev. Prof. JOHNSON, M.A., Rev. A. ROWLAND, B.A., LL.B., Rev. A. MUIR, and Rev. R. GREEN. Fifth Edition. 2 vols., 21s.

The Acts of the Apostles. By the Bishop of Bath and Wells. With Homilies by Rev. Prof. P. C. BARKER, M.A., LL.B., Rev. Prof. E. JOHNSON, M.A., Rev. Prof. R. A. REDFORD, M.A., Rev. R. TUCK, B.A., Rev. W. CLARKSON, B.A. Third Edition. 2 vols., 21s.

I. Corinthians. By the Ven. Archdeacon FARRAR, D.D. With Homilies by Rev. Ex-Chancellor LIPSCOMB, LL.D., Rev. DAVID THOMAS, D.D., Rev. D. FRASER, D.D., Rev. Prof. J. R. THOMSON, M.A., Rev. J. WAITE, B.A., Rev. R. TUCK, B.A., Rev. E. HURNDALL, M.A., and Rev. H. BREMNER, B.D. Third Edition. Price 15s.

II. Corinthians and Galatians. By the Ven. Archdeacon FARRAR, D.D., and Rev. Preb. E. HUXTABLE. With Homilies by Rev. Ex-Chancellor LIPSCOMB, LL.D., Rev. DAVID THOMAS, D.D., Rev. DONALD FRASER, D.D., Rev. R. TUCK, B.A., Rev. E. HURNDALL, M.A., Rev. Prof. J. R. THOMSON, M.A., Rev. R. FINLAYSON, B.A., Rev. W. F. ADENEY, M.A., Rev. R. M. EDGAR, M.A., and Rev. T. CROSKERRY, D.D. Price 21s.

Pulpit Commentary, The. (New Testament Series.)—*continued.*

Ephesians, Phillipians, and Colossians. By the Rev. Prof. W. G. BLAIKIE, D.D., Rev. B. C. CAFFIN, M.A., and Rev. G. G. FINDLAY, B.A. With Homilies by Rev. D. THOMAS, D.D., Rev. R. M. EDGAR, M.A., Rev. R. FINLAYSON, B.A., Rev. W. F. ADENEY, M.A., Rev. Prof. T. CROSKERRY, D.D., Rev. E. S. PROUT, M.A., Rev. Canon VERNON HUTTON, and Rev. U. R. THOMAS, D.D. Price 21s.

Hebrews and James. By the Rev. J. BARNBY, D.D., and Rev. Prebendary E. C. S. GIBSON, M.A. With Homiletics by the Rev. C. JERDAN, M.A., LL.B., and Rev. Prebendary E. C. S. GIBSON. And Homilies by the Rev. W. JONES, Rev. C. NEW, Rev. D. YOUNG, B.A., Rev. J. S. BRIGHT, Rev. T. F. LOCKYER, B.A., and Rev. C. JERDAN, M.A., LL.B. Price 15s.

PUNCHARD, E. G., D.D.—**Christ of Contention.** Three Essays. Fcap. 8vo, 2s.

PUSEY, Dr.—**Sermons for the Church's Seasons from Advent to Trinity.** Selected from the Published Sermons of the late EDWARD BOUVERIE PUSEY, D.D. Crown 8vo, 5s.

RANKE, Leopold von.—**Universal History.** The oldest Historical Group of Nations and the Greeks. Edited by G. W. PROTHERO. Demy 8vo, 16s.

RENDELL, J. M.—**Concise Handbook of the Island of Madeira.** With Plan of Funchal and Map of the Island. Fcap. 8vo, 1s. 6d.

REYNOLDS, Rev. J. W.—**The Supernatural in Nature.** A Verification by Free Use of Science. Third Edition, Revised and Enlarged. Demy 8vo, 14s.

The Mystery of Miracles. Third and Enlarged Edition. Crown 8vo, 6s.

The Mystery of the Universe; Our Common Faith. Demy 8vo, 14s.

RIBOT, Prof. Th.—**Heredity:** A Psychological Study on its Phenomena, its Laws, its Causes, and its Consequences. Second Edition. Large crown 8vo, 9s.

RIMMER, William, M.D.—**Art Anatomy.** A Portfolio of 81 Plates. Folio, 70s., nett.

ROBERTSON, The late Rev. F. W., M.A.—**Life and Letters of.** Edited by the Rev. STOPFORD BROOKE, M.A.

    I. Two vols., uniform with the Sermons. With Steel Portrait. Crown 8vo, 7s. 6d.

    II. Library Edition, in Demy 8vo, with Portrait. 12s.

    III. A Popular Edition, in 1 vol. Crown 8vo, 6s.

Sermons. Four Series. Small crown 8vo, 3s. 6d. each.

The Human Race, and other Sermons. Preached at Cheltenham, Oxford, and Brighton. New and Cheaper Edition. Small crown 8vo, 3s. 6d.

ROBERTSON, The late Rev. F. W., M.A.—continued.

Notes on Genesis. New and Cheaper Edition. Small crown 8vo, 3s. 6d.

Expository **Lectures on St. Paul's Epistles to the** Corinthia**ns.** A New Edition. Small crown 8vo, 5s.

Lectures **and Addresses,** with other Literary Remains. A New Edition. Small crown 8vo, 5s.

An Analysis of Tennyson's "In Memoriam." (Dedicated by Permission to the Poet-Laureate.) Fcap. 8vo, 2s.

The Education of the Human Race. Translated from the German of GOTTHOLD EPHRAIM LESSING. Fcap. 8vo, 2s. 6d.

The above Works can also be had, bound in half morocco.
, A Portrait of the late Rev. F. W. Robertson, mounted for framing, can be had, 2s. 6d.

ROMANES, G. J.— Mental Evolution in **Anim**als. With a Posthumous Essay on Instinct by CHARLES DARWIN, F.R.S. Demy 8vo, 12s.

ROOSEVELT, Theodore. **Hun**ting Trips **of a Ranchman.** Sketches of Sport on the Northern Cattle Plains. With 26 Illustrations. Royal 8vo, 18s.

Rosmini's Origin of Ideas. Translated from the Fifth Italian Edition of the Nuovo Saggio *Sull' origine delle idee.* 3 vols. Demy 8vo, cloth, 16s. each.

Rosmini's **Psychology.** 3 vols. Demy 8vo. [Vols. I. and II. now ready, 16s. each.

Rosmini's Philosophical System. Translated, with a Sketch of the Author's Life, Bibliography, Introduction, and Notes by THOMAS DAVIDSON. Demy 8vo, 16s.

RULE, Martin, M.A.— **The Life and Times of St. Anselm,** Archbishop **of Canterbury and Primate of the Britains.** 2 vols. Demy 8vo, 32s.

*SAMUEL, Sydney M.—***Jewish Life in the East.** Small crown 8vo, 3s. 6d.

*SARTORIUS, Ernestine.—***Three Months in the Soudan.** With 11 Full-page Illustrations. Demy 8vo, 14s.

*SAYCE, Rev. Archibald Henry.—***Introduction to the** Science **of Language.** 2 vols. Second Edition. Large post 8vo, 21s.

*SCOONES, W. Baptiste.—***Four Centuries of English Letters:** A Selection of 350 Letters by 150 Writers, from the Period of the Paston Letters to the Present Time. Third Edition. Large crown 8vo, 6s.

*SÉE, Prof. Germain.—***Bacillary Phthisis of the Lungs.** Translated and edited for English Practitioners by WILLIAM HENRY WEBER, M.R.C.S. Demy 8vo, 10s. 6d.

Shakspere's Works. The Avon Edition, 12 vols., fcap. 8vo, cloth, 18s. ; in cloth box, 21s. ; bound in 6 vols., cloth, 15s.

SHILLITO, Rev. Joseph.—Womanhood : its Duties, Temptations, and Privileges. A Book for Young Women. Third Edition. Crown 8vo, 3s. 6d.

SIDNEY, Algernon.—A Review. By GERTRUDE M. IRELAND BLACKBURNE. Crown 8vo, 6s.

Sister Augustine, Superior of the Sisters of Charity at the St. Johannis Hospital at Bonn. Authorised Translation by HANS THARAU, from the German "Memorials of AMALIE VON LASAULX." Cheap Edition. Large crown 8vo, 4s. 6d.

SKINNER, James.—A Memoir. By the Author of "Charles Lowder." With a Preface by the Rev. Canon CARTER, and Portrait. Large crown, 7s. 6d.
  *** Also a cheap Edition. With Portrait. Crown 8vo, 3s. 6d.

SMITH, Edward, M.D., LL.B., F.R.S.—Tubercular Consumption in its Early and Remediable Stages. Second Edition. Crown 8vo, 6s.

SMITH, Sir W. Cusack, Bart.—Our War Ships. A Naval Essay. Crown 8vo, 5s.

Spanish Mystics. By the Editor of " Many Voices." Crown 8vo, 5s.

Specimens of English Prose Style from Malory to Macaulay. Selected and Annotated, with an Introductory Essay, by GEORGE SAINTSBURY. Large crown 8vo, printed on hand-made paper, parchment antique or cloth, 12s. ; vellum, 15s.

SPEDDING, James.—Reviews and Discussions, Literary, Political, and Historical not relating to Bacon. Demy 8vo, 12s. 6d.

  Evenings with a Reviewer; or, Macaulay and Bacon. With a Prefatory Notice by G. S. VENABLES, Q.C. 2 vols. Demy 8vo, 18s.

STAPFER, Paul.—Shakespeare and Classical Antiquity : Greek and Latin Antiquity as presented in Shakespeare's Plays. Translated by EMILY J. CAREY. Large post 8vo, 12s.

STATHAM, F. Reginald.—Free Thought and Truth Thought. A Contribution to an Existing Argument. Crown 8vo, 6s.

STEVENSON, Rev. W. F.—Hymns for the Church and Home. Selected and Edited by the Rev. W. FLEMING STEVENSON.
  The Hymn Book consists of Three Parts :—I. For Public Worship.—II. For Family and Private Worship.—III. For Children. SMALL EDITION. Cloth limp, 10d. ; cloth boards, 1s. LARGE TYPE EDITION. Cloth limp, 1s. 3d. ; cloth boards, 1s. 6d.

Stray Papers on Education, and Scenes from School Life. By B. H. Second Edition. Small crown 8vo, 3s. 6d.

STREATFEILD, Rev. G. S., M.A.—Lincolnshire and the Danes. Large crown 8vo, 7s. 6d.

STRECKER-WISLICENUS.—**Organic Chemistry.** Translated and Edited, with Extensive Additions, by W. R. HODGKINSON, Ph.D., and A. J. GREENAWAY, F.I.C. Second and cheaper Edition. Demy 8vo, 12s. 6d.

Suakin, 1885; being a Sketch of the Campaign of this year. By an Officer who was there. Second Edition. Crown 8vo, 2s. 6d.

SULLY, James, M.A.—**Pessimism :** a History and a Criticism. Second Edition. Demy 8vo, 14s.

Sunshine and Sea. A Yachting Visit to the Channel Islands and Coast of Brittany. With Frontispiece from a Photograph and 24 Illustrations. Crown 8vo, 6s.

SWEDENBORG, Eman.—**De Cultu et Amore Dei ubi Agitur de Telluris ortu, Paradiso et Vivario, tum de Primogeniti Seu Adami Nativitate Infantia, et Amore.** Crown 8vo, 6s.

> **On the Worship and Love of God.** Treating of the Birth of the Earth, Paradise, and the Abode of Living Creatures. Translated from the original Latin. Crown 8vo, 7s. 6d.

> **Prodromus Philosophiæ Ratiocinantis de Infinito, et Causa Finali Creationis ;** deque Mechanismo Operationis Animæ et Corporis. Edidit THOMAS MURRAY GORMAN, M.A. Crown 8vo, 7s. 6d.

TACITUS.—**The Agricola.** A Translation. Small crown 8vo, 2s. 6d.

TAYLOR, Rev. Isaac.—**The Alphabet.** An Account of the Origin and Development of Letters. With numerous Tables and Facsimiles. 2 vols. Demy 8vo, 36s.

TAYLOR, Jeremy.—**The Marriage Ring.** With Preface, Notes, and Appendices. Edited by FRANCIS BURDETT MONEY COUTTS. Small crown 8vo, 2s. 6d.

TAYLOR, Sedley.—**Profit Sharing between Capital and Labour.** To which is added a Memorandum on the Industrial Partnership at the Whitwood Collieries, by ARCHIBALD and HENRY BRIGGS, with remarks by SEDLEY TAYLOR. Crown 8vo, 2s. 6d.

"They Might Have Been Together Till the Last." An Essay on Marriage, and the position of Women in England. Small crown 8vo, 2s.

Thirty Thousand Thoughts. Edited by the Rev. CANON SPENCE, Rev. J. S. EXELL, and Rev. CHARLES NEIL. 6 vols. Super royal 8vo.

> [Vols. I.-IV. now ready, 16s. each.

THOM, J. Hamilton.—**Laws of Life after the Mind of Christ.** Two Series. Crown 8vo, 7s. 6d. each.

THOMPSON, Sir H.—**Diet in Relation to Age and Activity.** Fcap. 8vo, cloth, 1s. 6d. ; Paper covers, 1s.

TIPPLE, Rev. S. A.—Sunday Mornings at Norwood. Prayers and Sermons. Crown 8vo, 6s.

TODHUNTER, Dr. J.—A Study of Shelley. Crown 8vo, 7s.

TOLSTOI, Count Leo.—Christ's Christianity. Translated from the Russian. Large crown 8vo, 7s. 6d.

TRANT, William.—Trade Unions: Their Origin, Objects, and Efficacy. Small crown 8vo, 1s. 6d.; paper covers, 1s.

TREMENHEERE, Hugh Seymour, C.B.—A Manual of the Principles of Government, as set forth by the Authorities of Ancient and Modern Times. New and Enlarged Edition. Crown 8vo, 3s. 6d. Cheap Edition, limp cloth, 1s.

TRENCH, The late R. C., Archbishop.—Notes on the Parables of Our Lord. Fourteenth Edition. 8vo, 12s.

Notes on the Miracles of Our Lord. Twelfth Edition. 8vo, 12s.

Studies in the Gospels. Fifth Edition, Revised. 8vo, 10s. 6d.

Brief Thoughts and Meditations on Some Passages in Holy Scripture. Third Edition. Crown 8vo, 3s. 6d.

Synonyms of the New Testament. Ninth Edition, Enlarged. 8vo, 12s.

Selected Sermons. Crown 8vo, 6s.

On the Authorized Version of the New Testament. Second Edition. 8vo, 7s.

Commentary on the Epistles to the Seven Churches in Asia. Fourth Edition, Revised. 8vo, 8s. 6d.

The Sermon on the Mount. An Exposition drawn from the Writings of St. Augustine, with an Essay on his Merits as an Interpreter of Holy Scripture. Fourth Edition, Enlarged. 8vo, 10s. 6d.

Shipwrecks of Faith. Three Sermons preached before the University of Cambridge in May, 1867. Fcap. 8vo, 2s. 6d.

Lectures on Mediæval Church History. Being the Substance of Lectures delivered at Queen's College, London. Second Edition. 8vo, 12s.

English, Past and Present. Thirteenth Edition, Revised and Improved. Fcap. 8vo, 5s.

On the Study of Words. Nineteenth Edition, Revised. Fcap. 8vo, 5s.

Select Glossary of English Words Used Formerly in Senses Different from the Present. Fifth Edition, Revised and Enlarged. Fcap. 8vo, 5s.

Proverbs and Their Lessons. Seventh Edition, Enlarged. Fcap. 8vo, 4s.

Poems. Collected and Arranged anew. Ninth Edition. Fcap. 8vo, 7s. 6d.

TRENCH, *The late R. C., Archbishop.—continued.*

Poems. Library Edition. 2 vols. Small crown 8vo, 10s.

Sacred Latin Poetry. Chiefly Lyrical, Selected and Arranged for Use. Third Edition, Corrected and Improved. Fcap. 8vo, 7s.

A Household **Book of English Poetry.** Selected and Arranged, with Notes. Fourth Edition, Revised. Extra fcap. 8vo, 5s. 6d.

An **Essay on the Life and Genius of Calderon.** With Translations from his "Life's a Dream" and "Great Theatre of the World." Second Edition, Revised and Improved. Extra fcap. 8vo, 5s. 6d.

Gustavus Adolphus in Germany, and other Lectures **on the Thirty Years'** War. Second Edition, Enlarged. Fcap. 8vo, 4s.

Plutarch; his Life, his **Lives, and** his Morals. Second Edition, Enlarged. Fcap. 8vo, 3s. 6d.

Remains **of** the late Mrs. Richard Trench. Being Selections from her Journals, Letters, and other Papers. New and Cheaper Issue. With Portrait. 8vo, 6s.

TUKE, *Daniel Hack, M.D., F.R.C.P.* Chapters in the History of **the Insane in the** British Isles. With Four Illustrations. Large **crown** 8vo, 12s.

TWINING, *Louisa.*—Work**house Visiting and** Management during Twenty-Five **Years.** Small crown 8vo, 2s.

TYLER, *J.*—The Mystery **of Being: or,** What Do We **Know** ? Small crown 8vo, 3s. 6d.

VAUGHAN, *H. Halford.*—New **Readings and Renderings of** Shakespeare's **Tragedies.** 3 vols. Demy 8vo, 12s. 6d. **each.**

VILLARI, *Professor.* - Niccolò **Machiavelli** and his **Times.** Translated by LINDA VILLARI. 4 vols. Large post 8vo, 48s.

VILLIERS, *The Right Hon. C. P.*—Free Trade **Speeches** of. With Political Memoir. Edited by a Member **of the** Cobden Club. 2 vols. With Portrait. Demy 8vo, 25s.

⁂ People's Edition. 1 vol. Crown 8vo, limp cloth, 2s. 6d.

VOGT, *Lieut.-Col. Hermann.*—**The Egyptian War of 1882.** A translation. With Map and Plans. Large crown 8vo, 6s.

VOLCKXSOM, *E. W. v.*—**Catechism of Elementary Modern** Chemistry. Small crown 8vo, 3s.

WALLER, *Rev. C. B.*—**The** Apocalypse, reviewed under the **Light** of the **Doctrine of the** Unfolding Ages, **and the** Restitution of All Things. Demy 8vo, 12s.

The Bible **Record of** Creation viewed **in its** Letter and Spirit. Two Sermons preached at St. Paul's **Church,** Woodford Bridge. Crown 8vo, 1s. 6d.

WALPOLE, *Chas. George.*—**A Short History of Ireland from the Earliest Times to the Union with Great Britain.** With 5 Maps and Appendices. Second Edition. Crown 8vo, 6s.

WARD, *William George, Ph.D.*—**Essays on the Philosophy of Theism.** Edited, with an Introduction, by WILFRID WARD. 2 vols. Demy 8vo, 21s.

WARD, *Wilfrid.*—**The Wish to Believe.** A Discussion Concerning the Temper of Mind in which a reasonable Man should undertake Religious Inquiry. Small crown 8vo, 5s.

WARTER, *J. W.*—**An Old Shropshire Oak.** 2 vols. Demy 8vo, 28s.

WEDDERBURN, *Sir David, Bart., M.P.*—**Life of.** Compiled from his Journals and Writings by his sister, Mrs. E. H. PERCIVAL. With etched Portrait, and facsimiles of Pencil Sketches. Demy 8vo, 14s.

WEDMORE, *Frederick.*—**The Masters of Genre Painting.** With Sixteen Illustrations. Post 8vo, 7s. 6d.

WHITE, *R. E.*—**Recollections of Woolwich during the Crimean War and Indian Mutiny, and of the Ordnance and War Departments; together with complete Lists of Past and Present Officials of the Royal Arsenal, etc.** Crown 8vo, 2s. 6d.

WHITNEY, *Prof. William Dwight.*—**Essentials of English Grammar,** for the Use of Schools. Second Edition. Crown 8vo, 3s. 6d.

WHITWORTH, *George Clifford.*—**An Anglo-Indian Dictionary:** a Glossary of Indian Terms used in English, and of such English or other Non-Indian Terms as have obtained special meanings in India. Demy 8vo, cloth, 12s.

WILLIAMS, *Rowland, D.D.*—**Psalms, Litanies, Counsels, and Collects for Devout Persons.** Edited by his Widow. New and Popular Edition. Crown 8vo, 3s. 6d.

Stray Thoughts from the Note Books of the late Rowland Williams, D.D. Edited by his Widow. Crown 8vo, 3s. 6d.

WILSON, *Lieut.-Col. C. T.*—**The Duke of Berwick, Marshal of France, 1702-1734.** Demy 8vo, 15s.

WILSON, *Mrs. R. F.*—**The Christian Brothers.** Their Origin and Work. With a Sketch of the Life of their Founder, the Ven. JEAN BAPTISTE, de la Salle. Crown 8vo, 6s.

WOLTMANN, *Dr. Alfred, and* WOERMANN, *Dr. Karl.*—**History of Painting.** With numerous Illustrations. Vol. I. Painting in Antiquity and the Middle Ages. Medium 8vo, 28s., bevelled boards, gilt leaves, 30s. Vol. II. The Painting of the Renascence.

YOUMANS, Eliza A.—First Book of Botany. Designed to
   Cultivate the Observing Powers of Children. With 300
   Engravings. New and Cheaper Edition. Crown 8vo, 2s. 6d.

YOUMANS, Edward L., M.D.—A Class Book of Chemistry, on
   the Basis of the New System. With 200 Illustrations. Crown
   8vo, 5s.

THE INTERNATIONAL SCIENTIFIC SERIES.

I. Forms of Water: a Familiar Exposition of the Origin and
   Phenomena of Glaciers. By J. Tyndall, LL.D., F.R.S. With
   25 Illustrations. Ninth Edition. 5s.

II. Physics and Politics; or, Thoughts on the Application of the
   Principles of "Natural Selection" and "Inheritance" to Political
   Society. By Walter Bagehot. Seventh Edition. 4s.

III. Foods. By Edward Smith, M.D., LL.B., F.R.S. With numerous
   Illustrations. Eighth Edition. 5s.

IV. Mind and Body: the Theories of their Relation. By Alexander
   Bain, LL.D. With Four Illustrations. Seventh Edition. 4s.

V. The Study of Sociology. By Herbert Spencer. Twelfth
   Edition. 5s.

VI. On the Conservation of Energy. By Balfour Stewart, M.A.,
   LL.D., F.R.S. With 14 Illustrations. Sixth Edition. 5s.

VII. Animal Locomotion; or Walking, Swimming, and Flying. By
   J. B. Pettigrew, M.D., F.R.S., etc. With 130 Illustrations.
   Third Edition. 5s.

VIII. Responsibility in Mental Disease. By Henry Maudsley,
   M.D. Fourth Edition. 5s.

IX. The New Chemistry. By Professor J. P. Cooke. With 31
   Illustrations. Eighth Edition, remodelled and enlarged. 5s.

X. The Science of Law. By Professor Sheldon Amos. Sixth Edition.
   5s.

XI. Animal Mechanism: a Treatise on Terrestrial and Aerial Locomotion. By Professor E. J. Marey. With 117 Illustrations.
   Third Edition. 5s.

XII. The Doctrine of Descent and Darwinism. By Professor
   O. Schmidt. With 26 Illustrations. Sixth Edition. 5s.

XIII. The History of the Conflict between Religion and
   Science. By J. W. Draper, M.D., LL.D. Nineteenth Edition.
   5s.

XIV. Fungi: their Nature, Influences, Uses, etc. By M. C. Cooke,
   M.D., LL.D. Edited by the Rev. M. J. Berkeley, M.A., F.L.S.
   With numerous Illustrations. Third Edition. 5s.

XV. The Chemical Effects of Light and Photography. By Dr. Hermann Vogel. With 100 Illustrations. Fourth Edition. 5s.

XVI. The Life and Growth of Language. By Professor William Dwight Whitney. Fifth Edition. 5s.

XVII. Money and the Mechanism of Exchange. By W. Stanley Jevons, M.A., F.R.S. Seventh Edition. 5s.

XVIII. The Nature of Light. With a General Account of Physical Optics. By Dr. Eugene Lommel. With 188 Illustrations and a Table of Spectra in Chromo-lithography. Third Edition. 5s.

XIX. Animal Parasites and Messmates. By P. J. Van Beneden. With 83 Illustrations. Third Edition. 5s.

XX. Fermentation. By Professor Schutzenberger. With 28 Illustrations. Fourth Edition. 5s.

XXI. The Five Senses of Man. By Professor Bernstein. With 91 Illustrations. Fifth Edition. 5s.

XXII. The Theory of Sound in its Relation to Music. By Professor Pietro Blaserna. With numerous Illustrations. Third Edition. 5s.

XXIII. Studies in Spectrum Analysis. By J. Norman Lockyer, F.R.S. With six photographic Illustrations of Spectra, and numerous engravings on Wood. Third Edition. 6s. 6d.

XXIV. A History of the Growth of the Steam Engine. By Professor R. H. Thurston. With numerous Illustrations. Third Edition. 6s. 6d.

XXV. Education as a Science. By Alexander Bain, LL.D. Fifth Edition. 5s.

XXVI. The Human Species. By Professor A. de Quatrefages. Third Edition. 5s.

XXVII. Modern Chromatics. With Applications to Art and Industry. By Ogden N. Rood. With 130 original Illustrations. Second Edition. 5s.

XXVIII. The Crayfish : an Introduction to the Study of Zoology. By Professor T. H. Huxley. With 82 Illustrations. Fourth Edition. 5s.

XXIX. The Brain as an Organ of Mind. By H. Charlton Bastian, M.D. With numerous Illustrations. Third Edition. 5s.

XXX. The Atomic Theory. By Prof. Wurtz. Translated by G. Cleminshaw, F.C.S. Fourth Edition. 5s.

XXXI. The Natural Conditions of Existence as they affect Animal Life. By Karl Semper. With 2 Maps and 106 Woodcuts. Third Edition. 5s.

XXXII. General Physiology of Muscles and Nerves. By Prof. J. Rosenthal. Third Edition. With Illustrations. 5s.

D

LI. The Common Sense of the Exact Sciences. By the late William Kingdon Clifford. Second Edition. With 100 Figures. 5*s*.

LII. Physical Expression: Its Modes and Principles. By Francis Warner, M.D., F.R.C.P. With 50 Illustrations. 5*s*.

LIII. Anthropoid Apes. By Robert Hartmann. With 63 Illustrations. 5*s*.

LIV. The Mammalia in their Relation to Primæval Times. By Oscar Schmidt. With 51 Woodcuts. 5*s*.

LV. Comparative Literature. By H. Macaulay Posnett, LL.D. 5*s*.

LVI. Earthquakes and other Earth Movements. By Prof. John Milne. With 38 Figures. 5*s*.

LVII. Microbes, Ferments, and Moulds. By E. L. Trouessart. With 107 Illustrations. 5*s*.

MILITARY WORKS.

BRACKENBURY, Col. C. B., R.A.—**Military** Handbooks for Regimental Officers.

I. Military Sketching and Reconnaissance. By Col. F. J. Hutchison and Major H. G. MacGregor. Fourth Edition. With 15 Plates. Small crown 8vo, 4*s*.

II. **The** Elements of Modern Tactics Practically applied to English Formations. By Lieut.-Col. Wilkinson Shaw. Fifth Edition. With 25 Plates and Maps. Small crown 8vo, 9*s*.

III. Field Artillery. Its Equipment, Organization and Tactics. By Major Sisson C. Pratt, R.A. With 12 Plates. Second Edition. Small crown 8vo, 6*s*.

IV. The Elements of Military Administration. First Part: Permanent System of Administration. By Major J. W. Buxton. Small crown 8vo, 7*s*. 6*d*.

V. Military Law: Its Procedure and Practice. By Major Sisson C. Pratt, R.A. Second Edition. Small crown 8vo, 4*s*. 6*d*.

VI. Cavalry in Modern **War.** By Col. F. Chenevix Trench. Small crown 8vo, 6*s*.

VII. Field Works. Their Technical Construction and Tactical Application. By the Editor, Col. C. B. Brackenbury, R.A. Small crown 8vo.

BRENT, Brig.-Gen. J. L.—Mobilizable Fortifications and their Controlling **Influence in** War. Crown 8vo, 5*s*.

POETRY.

BLUNT, Wilfred Scawen—continued.
  The Love Sonnets of Proteus. Fifth Edition, 18mo. Cloth extra, gilt top, 5s.

BOWEN, H. C., M.A.—Simple English Poems. English Literature for Junior Classes. In Four Parts. Parts I., II., and III., 6d. each, and Part IV., 1s. Complete, 3s.

BRYANT, W. C.—Poems. Cheap Edition, with Frontispiece. Small crown 8vo, 3s. 6d.

Calderon's Dramas: the Wonder-Working Magician—Life is a Dream—the Purgatory of St. Patrick. Translated by DENIS FLORENCE MACCARTHY. Post 8vo, 10s.

Camoens Lusiads.—Portuguese Text, with Translation by J. J. AUBERTIN. Second Edition. 2 vols. Crown 8vo, 12s.

CAMPBELL, Lewis.—Sophocles. The Seven Plays in English Verse. Crown 8vo, 7s. 6d.

CERVANTES. Journey to Parnassus. Spanish Text, with Translation into English Tercets, Preface, and Illustrative Notes, by James Y. Gibson. Crown 8vo, 12s.

  Numantia: a Tragedy. Translated from the Spanish, with Introduction and Notes, by JAMES Y. GIBSON. Crown 8vo, printed on hand-made paper, 5s.

CHAPMAN, Mary Charles.—A Few Translations from Victor Hugo and other Poets. Small crown 8vo, 2s. 6d.

CHEEVER, S. T.—The End of Man. With 4 Antique Illustrations. 4to, 10s. 6d.

Chronicles of Christopher Columbus. A Poem in 12 Cantos. By M. D. C. Crown 8vo, 7s. 6d.

CLARKE, Mary Cowden.—Honey from the Weed. Verses. Crown 8vo, 7s.

COXHEAD, Ethel.—Birds and Babies. Imp. 16mo. With 33 Illustrations. Gilt, 2s. 6d.

DE BÉRANGER.—A Selection from his Songs. In English Verse. By WILLIAM TOYNBEE. Small crown 8vo, 2s. 6d.

DENNIS, J.—English Sonnets. Collected and Arranged by. Small crown 8vo, 2s. 6d.

DE VERE, Aubrey.—Poetical Works.
  I. THE SEARCH AFTER PROSERPINE, etc. 6s.
  II. THE LEGENDS OF ST. PATRICK, etc. 6s.
  III. ALEXANDER THE GREAT, etc. 6s.

  The Foray of Queen Meave, and other Legends of Ireland's Heroic Age. Small crown 8vo, 5s.

  Legends of the Saxon Saints. Small crown 8vo, 6s.

DOBSON, Austin.—Old World Idylls and other Verses. Sixth Edition. Elzevir 8vo, gilt top, 6s.

At the Sign of the Lyre. Fourth Edition. Elzevir 8vo, gilt top, 6s.

DOMETT, Alfred.—Ranolf and Amohia. A Dream of Two Lives. New Edition, Revised. 2 vols. Crown 8vo, 12s.

Dorothy: a Country Story in Elegiac Verse. With Preface. Demy 8vo, 5s.

DOWDEN, Edward, LL.D.—Shakspere's Sonnets. With Introduction and Notes. Large post 8vo, 7s. 6s.

Dulce Cor: being the Poems of Ford Bereton. With Two Illustrations. Crown 8vo, 6s.

DUTT, Toru.—A Sheaf Gleaned in French Fields. New Edition. Demy 8vo, 10s. 6d.

Ancient Ballads and Legends of Hindustan. With an Introductory Memoir by EDMUND GOSSE. Second Edition. 18mo. Cloth extra, gilt top, 5s.

EDWARDS, Miss Betham.—Poems. Small crown 8vo, 3s. 6d.

ELDRYTH, Maud.—Margaret, and other Poems. Small crown 8vo, 3s. 6d.

All Soul's Eve, "No God," and other Poems. Fcap. 8vo, 3s. 6d.

ELLIOTT, Ebenezer, The Corn Law Rhymer.—Poems. Edited by his son, the Rev. EDWIN ELLIOTT, of St John's, Antigua. 2 vols. Crown 8vo, 18s.

English Verse. Edited by W. J. LINTON and R. H. STODDARD. 5 vols. Crown 8vo, cloth, 5s. each.
  I. CHAUCER TO BURNS.
  II. TRANSLATIONS.
  III. LYRICS OF THE NINETEENTH CENTURY.
  IV. DRAMATIC SCENES AND CHARACTERS.
  V. BALLADS AND ROMANCES.

ENIS.—Gathered Leaves. Small crown 8vo, 3s. 6d.

EVANS, Anne.—Poems and Music. With Memorial Preface by ANN THACKERAY RITCHIE. Large crown 8vo, 7s.

GOODCHILD, John A.—Somnia Medici. Two series. Small crown 8vo, 5s. each.

GOSSE, Edmund W.—New Poems. Crown 8vo, 7s. 6d.

Firdausi in Exile, and other Poems. Elzevir 8vo, gilt top, 6s.

GRINDROD, Charles.—Plays from English History. Crown 8vo, 7s. 6d.

The Stranger's Story, and his Poem, The Lament of Love: An Episode of the Malvern Hills. Small crown 8vo, 2s. 6d.

GURNEY, *Rev. Alfred.* —The Vision of the Eucharist, and other Poems. Crown 8vo, 5*s.*

A Christmas Faggot. Small crown 8vo, 5*s.*

HENRY, *Daniel, Junr.* —Under a Fool's Cap. Songs. Crown 8vo, cloth, bevelled boards, **5*s.***

HEYWOOD, *J. C.* —Herodias, a Dramatic Poem. **New** Edition, Revised. Small crown 8vo, 5*s.*

Antonius. A Dramatic Poem. New Edition, Revised. Small crown 8vo, 5*s.*

HICKEY, *E. H.* —**A Sculptor,** and other Poems. Small **crown** 8vo, **5*s.***

HOLE, *W. G.* — Procris, and other Poems. Fcap. 8vo, 3*s.* 6*d.*

KEATS, *John.* —Poetical Works. Edited by W. T. ARNOLD. Large crown 8vo, choicely printed on hand-made paper, with Portrait in *eau forte*. Parchment or cloth, 12*s.* : vellum, 15*s.*

KING, *Mrs. Hamilton.* —The Disciples. Eighth Edition, and Notes. Small crown 8vo, 5*s.*

A Book of Dreams. Crown 8vo, 3*s.* 6*d.*

KNOX, *The Hon. Mrs. O. N.* —Four Pictures from a Life, and other Poems. Small crown 8vo, 3*s.* 6*d.*

LANG, *A.* —XXXII Ballades in Blue China. Elzevir 8vo, 5*s.*

Rhymes à la Mode. With Frontispiece by E. A. Abbey. Elzevir 8vo, cloth extra, gilt top, 5*s.*

LAWSON, *Right Hon. Mr. Justice.* —Hymni Usitati Latine Redditi : with other Verses. Small 8vo, parchment, 5*s.*

Lessing's Nathan the Wise. Translated by EUSTACE K. CORBETT. Crown 8vo, 6*s.*

Life Thoughts. Small crown 8vo, 2*s.* 6*d.*

Living English Poets MDCCCLXXXII. With Frontispiece by Walter Crane. Second Edition. Large crown 8vo. Printed on hand-made paper. Parchment or cloth, 12*s.* ; vellum, 15*s.*

LOCKER, *F.* —London Lyrics. Tenth Edition. With Portrait, Elzevir 8vo. Cloth extra, gilt top, 5*s.*

Love in Idleness. A Volume of Poems. With an Etching by W. B. Scott. Small crown 8vo, 5*s.*

LUMSDEN, *Lieut.-Col. H. W.* —Beowulf : **an** Old English Poem. Translated into Modern Rhymes. Second and Revised Edition. Small crown 8vo. 5*s.*

LYSAGHT, *Sidney Royse.* —A Modern Ideal. A Dramatic Poem. Small crown 8vo, 5*s.*

MACGREGOR, *Duncan.* —Clouds and Sunlight. Poems. Small crown 8vo, 5*s.*

MAGNUSSON, Eirikr, M.A., and PALMER, E. H., M.A.—Johan Ludvig Runeberg's Lyrical Songs, Idylls, and Epigrams. Fcap. 8vo, 5s.

MAKCLOUD, Iren.—Ballads of the Western Highlands and Islands of Scotland. Small crown 8vo, 3s. 6d.

McNAUGHTON, J. H.—Onnalinda. A Romance. Small crown 8vo, 7s. 6d.

MEREDITH, Owen [The Earl of Lytton].—Lucile. New Edition. With 32 Illustrations. 16mo, 3s. 6d. Cloth extra, gilt edges, 4s. 6d.

MORRIS, Lewis.—Poetical Works of. New and Cheaper Editions, with Portrait. Complete in 3 vols., 5s. each.
    Vol. I. contains "Songs of Two Worlds." Eleventh Edition.
    Vol. II. contains "The Epic of Hades." Twentieth Edition.
    Vol. III. contains "Gwen" and "The Ode of Life." Sixth Edition.

    The Epic of Hades. With 16 Autotype Illustrations, after the Drawings of the late George R. Chapman. 4to, cloth extra, gilt leaves, 21s.

    The Epic of Hades. Presentation Edition. 4to, cloth extra, gilt leaves, 10s. 6d.

    Songs Unsung. Fifth Edition. Fcap. 8vo, 5s.

    The Lewis Morris Birthda**y** Book. Edited by S. S. Copeman, with Frontispiece after a Design by the late George R. Chapman. 32mo, cloth extra, gilt edges, 2s.; cloth limp, 1s. 6d.

MORSHEAD, E. D. A.—The House of Atreus. Being the Agamemnon, Libation-Bearers, and Furies of Æschylus. Translated into English Verse. Crown 8vo, 7s.

    The Suppliant Maidens of Æschylus. Crown 8vo, 3s. 6d.

MOZLEY, J. Richard.—The Romance of Dennell. A Poem in Five Cantos. Crown 8vo, 7s. 6d.

MULHOLLAND, Rosa.—Vagrant Verses. Small crown 8vo, 5s.

NOEL, The Hon. Roden.—A Little Child's Monument. Third Edition. Small crown 8vo, 3s. 6d.

    The House of Ravensburg. New Edition. Small crown 8vo, 6s.

    The Red Flag, and other Poems. New Edition. Small crown 8vo, 6s.

    Songs of the Heights and **Deeps.** Crown 8vo, 6s.

O'HARA, Constance Mary.—Burley Bells. Small crown 8vo, 3s. 6d.

O'HAGAN, John.—The Song of Roland. Translated into English Verse. New and Cheaper Edition. Crown 8vo, 5s.

PFEIFFER, Emily.—The Rhyme of the Lady of the Rock, and How it Grew. Second Edition. Small crown 8vo, 3s. 6d.

PFEIFFER, Emily—continued.

Gerard's Monument, **and other Poems.** Second Edition. Crown 8vo, 6s.

Under the Aspens: Lyrical and **Dramatic. With Portrait.** Crown 8vo, 6s.

PLATT, J. J.—Idyls and Lyrics of the Ohio Valley. Crown 8vo, 5s.

PLATT, Sarah M. B.—**A** Voyage to the Fortunate Isles, and other Poems. 1 vol. Small crown 8vo, gilt top, 5s.

In Primrose Time. A New Irish Garland. Small crown 8vo, 2s. 6d.

Rare Poems of the 16th and 17th Centuries. Edited **W. J.** LINTON. Crown 8vo, 5s.

RHOADES, James.—The Georgics **of Virgil.** Translated into English Verse. Small crown 8vo, **5s.**
Poems. Small crown 8vo, 4s. 6d.

ROBINSON, A. Mary F.—A Handful **of** Honeysuckle. Fcap. 8vo, 3s. 6d.

The Crowned Hippolytus. Translated from Euripides. With New Poems. Small crown 8vo, 5s.

ROUS, Lieut.-Col.—Conradin. Small crown 8vo, 2s.

SAUNDS, R. H. Egeus, and other Poems. Small crown 8vo, 3s. 6d.

SCHILLER, Friedrich. Wallenstein. A Drama. Done in English Verse, by J. A. W. HUNTER, M.A. Crown 8vo, 7s. 6d.

SCOTT, E. J. L.—The Eclogues of Virgil.—Translated into English Verse. Small crown 8vo, 3s. 6d.

SCOTT, George F. E.—Theodora and other **Poems. Small** crown 8vo, 3s. 6d.

SEYMOUR, F. H. A.—Rienzi. A Play in Five Acts. Small crown 8vo, 5s.

Shakspere's Works. The Avon Edition, 12 vols., fcap. 8vo, cloth, 18s.; and in box, 21s.; bound in 6 vols., cloth, 15s.

SHERBROOKE, Viscount.—Poems of a Life. Second Edition. Small crown 8vo, 2s. 6d.

SMITH, J. W. Gilbart.—The Loves **of Vandyck.** A Tale of Genoa. Small crown 8vo, 2s. 6d.

The Log o' the "Norseman." Small crown 8vo, **5s.**

Songs of Coming Day. Small crown 8vo, **3s. 6d.**

Sophocles: The Seven Plays in English **Verse.** Translated **by LEWIS** CAMPBELL. Crown 8vo, **7s. 6d.**

SPICER, Henry.—Haska: a Drama in Three Acts (as represented at the Theatre Royal, Drury **Lane,** March 10th, **1877). Third** Edition. Crown 8vo, 3s. 6d.

Uriel Acosta, in Three Acts. **From the German of Gatzkow.** Small crown 8vo, 2s. 6d.

SYMONDS, John Addington.—Vagabunduli Libellus. Crown Svo, 6s.

Tasso's Jerusalem Delivered. Translated by Sir JOHN KINGSTON JAMES, Bart. Two Volumes. Printed on hand-made paper, parchment, bevelled boards. Large crown Svo, 21s.

TAYLOR, Sir H.—Works. Complete in Five Volumes. Crown Svo, 30s.

Philip Van Artevelde. Fcap. Svo, 3s. 6d.

The Virgin Widow, etc. Fcap. Svo, 3s. 6d.

The Statesman. Fcap. Svo, 3s. 6d.

TAYLOR, Augustus.—Poems. Fcap. Svo, 5s.

TAYLOR, Margaret Scott.—"Boys Together," and other Poems. Small crown Svo, 6s.

TODHUNTER, Dr. J.—Laurella, and other Poems. Crown Svo, 6s. 6d.

Forest Songs. Small crown Svo, 3s. 6d.

The True Tragedy of Rienzi: a Drama. 3s. 6d.

Alcestis: a Dramatic Poem. Extra fcap. Svo, 5s.

Helena in Troas. Small crown Svo, 2s. 6d.

TYLER, M. C.—Anne Boleyn. A Tragedy in Six Acts. Second Edition. Small crown Svo, 2s. 6d.

TYNAN, Katharine.—Louise de la Valliere, and other Poems. Small crown Svo, 3s. 6d.

WEBSTER, Augusta.—In a Day: a Drama. Small crown Svo, 2s. 6d.

Disguises: a Drama. Small crown Svo, 5s.

Wet Days. By a Farmer. Small crown Svo, 6s.

WOOD, Rev. F. H.—Echoes of the Night, and other Poems. Small crown Svo, 3s. 6d.

Wordsworth Birthday Book, The. Edited by ADELAIDE and VIOLET WORDSWORTH. 32mo, limp cloth, 1s. 6d.; cloth extra, 2s.

YOUNGMAN, Thomas George.—Poems. Small crown Svo, 5s.

YOUNGS, Ella Sharpe.—Paphus, and other Poems. Small crown Svo, 3s. 6d.

A Heart's Life, Sarpedon, and other Poems. Small crown Svo, 3s. 6d.

NOVELS AND TALES.

"All But:" a Chronicle of Laxenford Life. By PEN OLIVER, F.R.C.S. With 20 Illustrations. Second Edition. Crown Svo, 6s.

BANKS, Mrs. G. L.—God's Providence House. New Edition. Crown Svo, 3s. 6d.

CHICHELE, Mary.—Doing and Undoing. A Story. Crown Svo, 4s. 6d.

Danish Parsonage. By an Angler. Crown Svo, 6s.

HUNTER, *Hay.*—The Crime of Christmas Day. A Tale of the Latin Quarter. By the Author of "My Ducats and my Daughter." 1s.

HUNTER, *Hay, and* WHYTE, *Walter.*—My Ducats and My Daughter. New and Cheaper Edition. With Frontispiece. Crown 8vo, 6s.

Hurst and Hanger. A History in Two Parts. 3 vols. 31s. 6d.

INGELOW, *Jean.*—Off the Skelligs: a Novel. With Frontispiece. Second Edition. Crown 8vo, 6s.

JENKINS, *Edward.*—A Secret of Two Lives. Crown 8vo, 2s. 6d.

KIELLAND, *Alexander L.*—Garman and Worse. A Norwegian Novel. Authorized Translation, by W. W. Kettlewell. Crown 8vo, 6s.

MACDONALD, *G.*—Donal Grant. A Novel. Second Edition. With Frontispiece. Crown 8vo, 6s.

Castle Warlock. A Novel. Second Edition. With Frontispiece. Crown 8vo, 6s.

Malcolm. With Portrait of the Author engraved on Steel. Seventh Edition. Crown 8vo, 6s.

The Marquis of Lossie. Sixth Edition. With Frontispiece. Crown 8vo, 6s.

St. George and St. Michael. Fifth Edition. With Frontispiece. Crown 8vo, 6s.

What's Mine's Mine. Second Edition. With Frontispiece. Crown 8vo, 6s.

Annals of a Quiet Neighbourhood. Fifth Edition. With Frontispiece. Crown 8vo, 6s.

The Seaboard Parish: a Sequel to "Annals of a Quiet Neighbourhood." Fourth Edition. With Frontispiece. Crown 8vo, 6s.

Wilfred Cumbermede. An Autobiographical Story. Fourth Edition. With Frontispiece. Crown 8vo, 6s.

MALET, *Lucas.*—Colonel Enderby's Wife. A Novel. New and Cheaper Edition. With Frontispiece. Crown 8vo, 6s.

MULHOLLAND, *Rosa.*—Marcella Grace. An Irish Novel. Crown 8vo.

PALGRAVE, *W. Gifford.*—Hermann Agha: an Eastern Narrative. Third Edition. Crown 8vo, 6s.

SHAW, *Flora L.*—Castle Blair; a Story of Youthful Days. New and Cheaper Edition. Crown 8vo, 3s. 6d.

STRETTON, *Hesba.*—Through a Needle's Eye: a Story. New and Cheaper Edition, with Frontispiece. Crown 8vo, 6s.

TAYLOR, *Col. Meadows, C.S.I., M.R.I.A.*—Seeta: a Novel. With Frontispiece. Crown 8vo, 6s.

Tippoo Sultaun: a Tale of the Mysore War. With Frontispiece. Crown 8vo, 6s.

Ralph Darnell. With Frontispiece. Crown 8vo, 6s.

A Noble Queen. With Frontispiece. Crown 8vo, 6s.

The Confessions of a Thug. With Frontispiece. Crown 8vo, 6s.

Tara: a Mahratta Tale. With Frontispiece. Crown 8vo, 6s.

Within Sound of the Sea. With Frontispiece. Crown 8vo, 6s.

BOOKS FOR THE YOUNG.

Brave Men's **Footsteps.** A Book of Example and Anecdote for Young People. By the Editor of "Men who have Risen." With **4** Illustrations by C. Doyle. Eighth Edition. Crown 8vo, 3s. 6d.

COXHEAD, Ethel.—Birds and Babies. Imp. 16mo. With 33 Illustrations. Cloth gilt, 2s. 6d.

DAVIES, G. Christopher.—Rambles and Adventures **of our** School Field Club. With 4 Illustrations. New and **Cheaper** Edition. Crown 8vo, 3s. 6d.

EDMONDS, Herbert.—Well Spent Lives : a Series **of** Modern Biographies. New and Cheaper Edition. Crown 8vo, 3s. 6d.

EVANS, Mark.—The Story of our Father's Love, told to Children. Sixth and Cheaper Edition of Theology for Children. With 4 Illustrations. Fcap. 8vo, 1s. 6d.

JOHNSON, Virginia W.—The Catskill Fairies. Illustrated by Alfred Fredericks. **5s.**

MACKENNA, S. J.—Plucky Fellows. A **Book** for Boys. With 6 Illustrations. Fifth Edition. Crown 8vo, 3s. 6d.

KEARY, Mrs. G. S.—Waking and Working ; or, From Girlhood to Womanhood. New and Cheaper Edition. With a Frontispiece. Crown 8vo, 3s. 6d.

    Blessing and Blessed : a Sketch **of** Girl Life. New and Cheaper Edition. Crown 8vo, 3s. 6d.

    Rose Gurney's Discovery. A Story **for** Girls. Dedicated to their Mothers. Crown 8vo, 3s. 6d.

    English Girls : Their Place and Power. With Preface by the Rev. R. W. Dale. Fourth Edition. Fcap. 8vo, 2s. 6d.

    Just Anyone, and other Stories. Three Illustrations. **Royal** 16mo, 1s. 6d.

    Sunbeam Willie, and other Stories. Three Illustrations. **Royal** 16mo, 1s. 6d.

    Sunshine Jenny, and other Stories. Three Illustrations. **Royal** 16mo, 1s. 6d.

STOCKTON, Frank R.—A **Jolly Fellowship.** With **20** Illustrations. Crown 8vo, 5s.

STORR, Francis, and TURNER, Hawes.—Canterbury Chimes ; or, Chaucer Tales re-told to Children. With 6 Illustrations from the Ellesmere Manuscript. Third Edition. Fcap. 8vo, 3s. 6d.

STRETTON, Hesba.—David **Lloyd's Last Will.** With **4** Illustrations. New Edition. Royal 16mo, 2s. 6d.

WHITAKER, Florence.—Christy's Inheritance. A London Story. Illustrated. Royal 16mo, 1s. 6d.

PRINTED BY WILLIAM CLOWES AND SONS, LIMITED, LONDON AND BECCLES.

www.ingramcontent.com/pod-product-compliance
Lightning Source LLC
Chambersburg PA
CBHW020227030726
47497CB00009B/2983